YOUNG DUMB
AND Vyce's Getback

DUCK SANCHEZ

READ THE YOUNG AND DUMB SERIES IN THIS ORDER

EBOOKS:
Young & Dumb
Young & Dumb 2 – The Finale
Young & Dumb: Vyce's Getback

OR

PAPERBACKS:
Young & Dumb: The Complete Series
Young & Dumb: Vyce's Getback: The Complete Series

Library of Congress Control Number: 2013947054
ISBN 10: 0989084574

ISBN 13: 9780989084574

Cover Design: Davida Baldwin www.oddballdsgn.com
Graphics: Davida Baldwin
www.thecartelpublications.com
First Edition

Printed in the United States of America

ARE YOU ON OUR EMAIL LIST?

CHECK OUT OTHER TITLES BY
THE CARTEL PUBLICATIONS

What's Up Fam,

This has been a busy summer! Not only are we still dropping novel after novel, we have also attended book fairs and film festivals. We are committed to bring you story telling in all avenues possible, including movies. Continue to rock with The Cartel Publications, we not keeping up with the majors, we are The Majors.

Now onto the book in hand, "Young & Dumb:Vyce's Getback". This novel is the follow up to the original, "Young & Dumb". Duck Sanchez comes right back at you with more craziness and drama filled antics of Bobbie & Claire; plus, some new fools are added to the insane mix. So buckle up, this story is bound to give you a wild ride.

Keeping in line with tradition, we want to give respect to a trailblazer paving the way. With that said we would like to recognize:

Dr. Dennis Kimbro

Dennis Kimbro is the author of, "Think and Grow Rich: A Black Choice" and "The Wealth Choice: Success Secrets of Black Millionaires". Dr. Kimbro helps the African-American community understand wealth and the road to success and fortune, and we appreciate all that he does.

Ok, go 'head and dive in! I'll get at you in the next novel.

Be Easy!
Charisse "C. Wash" Washington
Vice President
The Cartel Publications
www.thecartelpublications.com
www.twitter.com/cartelbooks
www.facebook.com/cartelpublications
Instagram: Cartelpublications

CHAPTER 1

BOBBI

O nce upon a time in a small W ashington
D . C . apartment...

A cold chill rolled through Red's dark bedroom, and slow music boomed from the speaker on the table as Bobbi fucked the shit out of her ex-boyfriend Red.

"Come on, Red, beat that pussy, baby," Bobbi said as she rode his dick hard. "Make me feel it, nigga. Make me feel it like you use to. I want you to stuff that thing all the way up in me." She was being extra dirty in the mouth and he loved it.

Red's tongue hung out of the side of his mouth as he pawed her titties, scratching them along the way with his nails. "Damn, Bobbi, that pussy still tight the way it use to be. Ain't nobody fucking this thang the way I do right? I can tell."

"No, Red, you got this shit all the way down, baby," she responded as she continued to grind on top of him. "It's yours...work it."

"Not that bitch either right?"

"Fuck that bitch," Bobbi professed, as she looked into his eyes. She wanted him to know that what she was about to say was real. "Claire can't satisfy me 1% of what you do." She bucked her hips wider and harder, so that all of his dick could fill her up. "I tell you that all the time, but now I want to show you." Bobbi slobbed him down and sucked his tongue.

Bobbi was wrong on many levels for sleeping with Red, but in all honesty she didn't give a fuck. She looked at the relationship she had with him as food to keep her situation alive with Claire. In her mind, he was a good thing not bad. Besides, at night she played the good wife to Claire who took care of her baby and cleaned house, but in the afternoons she burned the highway with her Benz from Delaware to DC, just to get up under him, and to be in his presence. If Red wasn't in her life, there would be no Claire. She needed balance.

She didn't have the slightest amount of remorse for how she was treating Claire. Besides, Bobbi wasn't with the gay shit on a regular basis anyway. If only she felt comfortable enough telling her part time lover how she really felt things would be sweet. Bobbi was only doing the relationship thing because Claire was a caregiver, and with her in the picture she had a live in babysitter for Tristan. No. Claire could keep her lesbian dreams to herself for all she cared. Bobbi was all about that good dick. Red's dick, and she wasn't letting anybody come in between that, not even Claire.

7

After he burst his cream into Bobbi's pussy, and she squeezed it into her body as if she were trying to have another baby, he kissed her softly on the lips.

"Why you doing this to me," he asked, rubbing her hair backwards. "You got my head twisted, and shit. That pussy feels like it came fresh out of the box."

"Red, you be talking that good stuff but you confuse me sometimes," she responded, trying not to breathe into his face after the fuck session they just had. "I mean one minute you throwing my clothes out in front of your apartment building, while everybody is outside watching, and the next minute you're telling me you love me. You got me messed up right now."

"I do love you, Bobbi. I'm being real with you."

"But what changed all of a sudden?"

Red sat on the edge of the bed and looked back at her sweaty body. Bobbi was beautiful no doubt. Her auburn hair was pulled back into a ponytail and her brown skin seemed to sparkle under the light. Bobbi was bad as shit. But there was just one thing wrong with her, and it was that she was selfish, loud, rude and a horrible person and mother. He couldn't trust Bobbi as far as he could throw her, no matter what he said to her when they were in the throws of fucking. Which was why it was crazy that she was even in his bed, considering how he treated her.

Two years ago when Bobbi met Vyce Anderson, when she was at her worst. She met Vyce on the street

8

one day after Red, the man whose bed she shared at the moment, threw her things out because she rummaged through his phone while he was in the shower and got caught. After a night of passion in the hotel with Vyce, she learned she was pregnant. The only thing was that although she told Vyce he was the father, she actually had sex with Red earlier that day, which resulted in Red being the true father of her baby, despite what she told Vyce.

At first Vyce wasn't on the baby tip until he realized it was cheaper to keep her, instead of risking her taking him to child support court. There was just one problem with Vyce's plan, he impregnated Claire, who was Bobbi's current live in lover.

At first Claire and Bobbi were at each other's throats when Vyce had the bright idea to move them both into his house. But after being shot, beaten and emotionally abused by Vyce, Claire and Bobbi came up with a scheme that allowed them both to get away with over three hundred thousand dollars of his money. Not only did they yank his bank account hard, Claire also killed his best friend Whiz after discovering that he might be on to them.

Immediately after the heist, they made a decision to leave Washington DC, buy a home in Delaware together and be in a sexual relationship. Since Claire lost her baby during the time she lived with Vyce, she took to Bobbi's baby and nurtured and loved him from the day he was born. But with all of the love and appreciation Claire had for them, Bobbi could never get over the fact that Claire was a woman, and she preferred men.

"Bobbi, I'm going to be real with you," Red said rubbing her clammy arm. "I wasn't thinking about you at first. To be honest, remember the day we broke up when I caught you going through my phone? Well that was it for me. I had to put you out, because I got tired of the lies and the sneaky shit. But, and this is also true, when you stopped calling me I started missing you a lot. I use to be mad as shit thinking that another dude was fucking you, and my heart couldn't take it."

"But when you had me you didn't want to be bothered, Red. I know you're saying that you missed me but it seems so out of place right now. Like it's not real."

He frowned. "How come you don't trust people?"

"Because everyone I trusted gave me a reason to realize why I shouldn't. And I'm not going to lie, it's going to take a long time for me to love you again, but I want to."

"Then just—"

"EVERYBODY PUT YOUR FUCKING HANDS UP IN THE AIR," yelled someone in the living room.

"What the fuck," Red said as he jumped up to get his gun that was in the closet across from the bed.

It was too late because two masked men were already in the bedroom. One of them held a gun over top of Red's head. "Don't make another fucking move unless you don't want your dick or your life!"

My dick? Red thought. *What the fuck kind of robbery is this?*

Red stopped in place and raised his hands into the air. He wanted to live and decided to play it smart.

Bobbi was completely unraveled and was experiencing déjà vu. The last time she went through a robbery like this, she set the entire thing up. It was during the time when she had her cousin's friends break down the door of the house that she shared with Vyce and Claire. When the heist was over she had snatched thousands of dollars from Vyce, and split the cash with Claire and the goons. But this robbery was unplanned and as far as she knew Red wasn't sitting on dough. Besides, he constantly hit her up for money.

"I don't got no money in here, man," Red said raising his hands higher. "Honest. Whoever told ya'll I was sitting on paper lied."

"Then you got a problem," Stick Up Kid # 1 said. "Because we not leaving here without some cash."

Red looked as if he were about to piss on himself. He wasn't lying when he said he was broke, but he could tell they didn't want to hear it. Suddenly he remembered that Bobbi went to the bank earlier in the day so he said, "I ain't got no money but she holding

11

five hundred dollars. Its in her purse over on the counter," he nodded.

Bobbi's eyes widened. "Red, what the fuck is wrong with you? That's the money for my mortgage!"

"Sorry, baby girl," he shrugged. "But this situation trumps your living arrangements now don't you agree?"

After they grabbed her purse, and snatched the wallet out, they backed slowly out of the bedroom, with their guns still aimed and the money. "Good shit, nigga, luckily for you we came up on this paper, because this situation could've gotten ugly. Real ugly. Now keep your hands up. You and the bitch, before we change our minds and leave you sticky and flat on the floor."

****

After the robbers, who were dopeheads, got what they came for, they jumped into their car and sped away from the scene. "Can you believe that shit," Stick Up Kid # 1 said. "Man, I told you that nigga was sitting on a little dough."

"He wasn't sitting on shit, it was the bitch who looked out and had the cash," Stick Up Kid # 2 said.

"Who gives a fuck if it was her or him," he responded. "We came out good. So lets just go get a pack so we can be right for the rest of the night. If we hurry up we can hit my uncle next. He expecting a shipment of white girl and I know they gonna have money on the table. We gonna be good on dope for at least a month."

The moment they made it to the house and parked, they couldn't make it out of the car before they were staring down the barrels of three guns. But it was the fourth man who wasn't holding a weapon who caused their stomachs to rumble. They stuck him up earlier in the week and had no idea that they were spotted. It was time to pay the dope boy.

"Vyce, I…I'm sorry about that…uh…man," the first one was so horrified he forgot his native language was English.

"Man, it wasn't personal when we got you last week," Stick Up Kid #2 said, hoping he would show them mercy. "You good peoples with—"

Unfortunately for him his speech was halted when one of Vyce's goons blew off his facial features. Stick Up Kid #1 screamed until he was knocked over the cheek with one of the weapons.

"As you can see your friend is no longer with us," Vyce said when he was quieter. "Now if you can't come up with my money in the next two seconds, and I mean every dime ya'll got me for, you're going to be laying right next to him. Now where's my paper?"

The second robber quickly handed him the wallet he stole from Bobbi. "That's all I got man. I swear to god that's it. I wouldn't even fuck around with you like that right now. I know you not playing."

"But you already did fuck me over," Vyce reminded him.

"It's money in that wallet, man, look inside of it. The least you could do is look and not kill me first."

Vyce scanned inside of the wallet quickly. "Fuck am I going to do with this? You got my man for a thousand."

"Well if you let me live I'll get the rest I swear to God. You know I'm sick with the hammer, Vyce. It won't take me more than twenty-four hours to come up with the rest of your paper. Just give me a chance. That's all I'm asking for."

Vyce already knew he was going to kill him. But to humor him, he opened the wallet fully to see how much money was really inside. His heart dropped when he saw Bobbi's face on the driver's license. He had been looking for her ever since she robbed and left him. He pulled it out and the wallet dropped out of his hand. "Where did you get this shit from?" he asked waving the license.

"From a nigga name Red. Well actually I didn't get it from the nigga, I got it from the bitch over his house."

"Do you know where he lives? Or did you hit him on the street?"

"I know exactly where that nigga lives."

Vyce tried hard not to show his pleasure. He had waited a long time to wrap his arms around Bobbi's

14

windpipe, because of the money she and Claire got him for, and now the moment had arrived.

"It looks like you were lucky enough to save your life after all."

CHAPTER 2

CLAIRE

Meanwhile in a half a million dollar home in Delaware...

"So the museum in Washington, D.C. can support fifty kids for Tristan's party, but I hope that's enough," Claire said to her mother Ricky as she sat in her own kitchen in Delaware, going over the details for the baby's birthday party.

Two-year-old Tristan sat on the floor playing with his rubber balls; oblivious to all the trouble Claire was going over for him.

"Claire, don't you think this is too expensive?" Ricky said observing the details on the papers in front of her. "For fifty kids at a museum you're going to pay about twenty five hundred dollars."

"Mommy, it's not about the dollar amount," Claire sighed as she walked to the refrigerator and grabbed two Coca-Cola's. "It's about the baby being happy." She placed her long curly hair behind her ear.

Ricky took the drink and leaned up against the counter to look at her daughter. "Claire, can I ask you something?" Her brown eyes were soft and it was obvious to Claire that whatever she wanted to ask was weighing on her heart. But, she didn't want to talk about her lifestyle either, because she knew her mother would never understand.

"Please don't go there right now, mama," she said grabbing the baby off the floor, before sitting on the bar stool by the counter with him. "I'm having a good day, and I don't feel like fighting with you."

"How do you know what I'm about to say?" Ricky frowned, rubbing the beautiful baby's curly hair, before pulling his red shirt over his huge belly-button. "You shouldn't assume."

"Because I know you, and you're my mother." Claire kissed Tristan on his puffy cheek and he awarded her with a toothless, juicy grin.

"If you know me so well then what was I about to say?" she crossed her arms over her chest.

"You were going to ask why am I watching the baby, when Bobbi is the mother, and she's always outside doing her thing."

"Claire, I wish that was the only thing I had to say to you. So as usual you got me all wrong."

Claire sighed. All of her life her mother made her feel like everything she did was dumb. She wouldn't tolerate Ricky so much if she weren't her best friend. But Claire was too weird and as a result, the only person, outside of her new associate Natalie, that she could talk to was her mother. She relied on her advice, even when Ricky didn't want to give it.

"Then what were you going to say, mama?"

"I was going to say that it's wrong how that girl does you, sweetheart. She rips and runs the streets while you sit here all day long watching her baby. You're nineteen years old, Claire. What happened to college? I mean you got a lovely house, even though I don't know how you got it, but this place still ain't enough. You need an education, because that's the only way you can truly survive in this world."

"Ma, please…" Claire rolled her eyes.

"Don't ma please me," Ricky frowned. "I'm serious. This house is only as good as the mortgage you can pay each month. You need an education if you want to live up to this lifestyle and it's time you start seeking college now."

Although Claire knew her mother was right about needing an education so that she could get a good job in order to keep her home, she didn't give her the particulars as to how she was able to afford such a lovely house either. She didn't tell Ricky that she robbed her ex-boyfriend alongside her new girlfriend Bobbi, to get the money to put a down payment on the home. Besides, she knew she'd never be able to handle it. Ricky wanted Claire to remain as pure as a newborn baby and that wasn't the case anymore. Claire had

18

seen too much. She'd been through too much and she would never be the same.

"I'm going back to school, ma, just not right now, okay? You need to relax."

"I'm not going to relax, Claire, you're my daughter. And if you not going to college now then when?"

"I'm waiting until the baby is at least in kindergarten. I want to make sure he's old enough to let me know if somebody is fucking with him. After that I'll go, but now is not the time."

"Claire, that's not your child," Ricky yelled. "Now I know you always wanted something to love—"

Claire frowned. "It's not a *something*, ma, it's a *baby*. And you're right, I love him very much, and I don't have to *want* him to love me because he already does. It's one thing for you not to understand my relationship with Bobbi, but it's a whole 'nother thing to bash me and Tristan."

"That's not what I mean, Claire. What I'm saying is that this gay shit you doing is going too far. You're playing daddy when you should be in school. I mean, how can you lay up with a woman everyday and not want a little something better? It plagues my mind."

"By better you mean dick?"

"Yes."

19

"Well I can do it real easy," Claire said in a sassy tone. "I haven't had my pussy licked so good in all of my life."

By the time Claire realized her mother had slapped her, the baby was crying in her lap. Claire calmly got up, walked him into the living room and placed him into his playpen where he stopped sobbing and occupied himself with his red ball. Slowly Claire walked back into the kitchen and addressed her mother.

"If you ever hit me again"— she pointed in her face— "I will never talk to you again, and I may hit you back."

Ricky stood silent for a moment. The idea of her daughter hitting her back hurt her feelings. "I'm sorry—"

Claire put her hand up silencing her mother immediately. "I don't want an apology, ma, I want an understanding. Because whether you realize it or not, I'm a grown woman and you can't come over my house and assault me and think I'm going to keep taking that shit."

"I'm sorry, baby," Ricky said filled with remorse. "I just want so much for you. I want you to have the life that I imagined, and this isn't it."

Although she didn't agree with her daughter's lifestyle, she could certainly see a change in Claire. It was all in her eyes and the way she held her head up. In the past Claire was timid and irresponsible. But now she could see that she was in control and speaking her mind in a way Ricky could respect. And Ricky was going to have to learn to deal with it if she wanted a relationship with her only child.

"It's cool, ma, but can you please leave my house now?" Claire could still feel the burn on her skin from where her mother just slapped her. "I really want to be alone."

"I understand." Ricky grabbed her purse and walked slowly toward the living room. Claire followed her and opened the front door. The moment Claire did she saw her friend Natalie Jennings from up the block, walking toward her house.

Ricky kissed her daughter on the cheek, smiled. "I really am, sorry, daughter."

"Bye, ma," Claire responded flatly. She watched her mother walk away.

Although Claire with her soft curly hair and taut body was attractive, Natalie on the other hand was drop dead gorgeous. Her dark chocolate skin and long silky black weave made her look doll-like. That is until you caught the curves of her tiny waist, thick ass and toned legs. Natalie Jennings was sexy and she knew it. She was also twenty-six years old, bored out of her mind and always looking for a way to get into trouble or somebody else's business.

"What's wrong with you?" Natalie asked walking into the house. "Your mother looked like she was upset too. Please don't tell me ya'll had a fight up in here." She looked around.

Claire closed the door and walked back into the living room to play with the baby. "Natalie you don't even know the half." She shook her head. "My mother…man…sometimes I can't stand her ass. She thinks I'm a fucking kid and I keep trying to tell her that I'm grown. Always in my business, always in my face, and always trying to tell me how to live my life."

Claire sat on the couch and pulled the playpen toward her just so she could rub on Tristan's head. Claire was the type of person who always had to be touching him all of the time. It was as if touching him made him realer, or more alive.

"Be easy, Claire. I know you mad and all, but you know you only get one mother in life," Natalie said tossing her purse on the sofa and sitting next to her. "Mothers don't want to run our lives, they just want the best for us, that's all. Give her a break."

Claire rolled her eyes. "That may be true but my mother is the fuck terrible." She shook her head. "I'm tired of her, Natalie. She always trying to run my life like I'm not old enough to do it myself. If she ain't talking about me and Tristan, and why I gotta be taking care of him all of the time, she talking about Bobbi. Although she might not understand my lifestyle it's still mine. All folks do when they bash people in gay relationships is push them away. And she about to not

22

have me in her life no more if she keep messing with
me."

When Natalie heard Bobbi's name she shook her
head and rolled her eyes.

"What's that all about?" Claire asked her. "I
know you not coming down on me about Bobbi again
too. Because I'm going to tell you like I told my mother, I'm not trying to hear it."

"I don't agree with your mother and how she be
coming at you about your relationship and all. I tell
folks all the time if you not fucking the person you
shouldn't be all concerned with what they doing in the
sheets, but she's right in some aspects, Claire."

"Aspects huh?" Claire sat back on the sofa. "Do
tell," she replied sarcastically, crossing her legs.

"Okay I will," she started. "First of all Bobbi's
freak-whore-ass needs to have several seats. She may
be a lot of things but in a relationship she's not, and
I'm just serving it to you straight."

Claire immediately grew angry and was thinking
about busting Natalie in her beautiful neck, but she
maintained her anger. Why were people always trying
to talk about Bobbi when they knew how she felt about
her?

"Fuck you trying to say, Natalie? And you
should know that if you lying all you gonna do is make
me mad as hell."

"I ain't trying to say nothing, and I'm not trying
to make you mad either. I'm flat out saying what it is.

23

Bobbi is a mess, Claire. And you need to leave her alone while you still can. That girl gonna either get you killed, caught with a STD, or left with a broken heart."

Natalie grabbed Tristan out of the pen and sat him on her lap. Although both she and Ricky didn't care for Bobbi, they would be lying if they didn't say he was the cutest baby they'd ever seen. Not only was he adorable, but he cried very little and was by all accounts a pleasure to be around. Everyone who knew Bobbi wondered how she didn't have the devil's spawn, instead of such a baby angel.

"I'm not leaving Bobbi, Natalie," Claire responded. "So you need to fix your lips up because you out of order right now. First of all even if somebody said Bobbi was out there living bad, I would give her the benefit of the doubt by asking her first. Second of all I know that girl wouldn't cheat on me. Not the way she calls my name in the bedroom, and how I take care of this house."

Natalie rolled her eyes. "Oh lawd," she paused. "I wasn't going to give it to you like this but I see now that you need to hear it hard." She positioned her body on the couch so that she was looking directly into her eyes. Tristan remained nestled in her lap. "You already know I'm from D.C., like you are. I never told you, but the only reason I bought a house out here was because I could get more house for my money. Anyway, when I was in the city getting up with my old friends earlier

24

today, I saw Bobbi in the car arguing with some fine ass red nigga in front of an apartment building. I'm talking about the battle was dead ass serious. They acted like they were a married couple or something. He was yanking her arm, and she was pulling away from him, it was all too fabulous of a performance for them not to be together."

Bobbi felt her heart stop. She couldn't believe what Natalie was actually implying. And in an effort to do something with her body, she pulled her knees into her chest and got to playing with her toes. It was a nervous reaction and she was quite aware that she looked stupid, but what Natalie was saying confused her.

Could Bobbi really be cheating? When she knew how much she cared about her?

"You lying," Claire said looking at Natalie play with the baby's fingers. "I know you lying."

"I'm not lying, and I know you know that. Bobbi is a freak, Claire, and you deserve better than her. Just stop fucking with her while you still can before things get worse between you two. Girl, I could never lay up with a person that did me publically the way she doing you. She don't respect ya'lls little thing. I'm just saying." She shrugged.

CHAPTER 3

VYCE

In a luxurious home in Washington D C ...

Tya was riding Vyce's dick on his bed as her body moved to the slow jams on the radio. Sweat dripped off of her breasts, and fell onto his chest, due to the heat being up so high. Vyce loved to fuck in the heat. Her long brown and black dreads were pulled up into a ponytail that sat on top of her head, and they moved every time she bucked her hips.

"I love you so much, Vyce," Tya said looking down into his eyes. "I didn't—"

Her statement was interrupted because Vyce hit her pleasure spot, and caused her to scream in pain/ecstasy. He loved how her face would distort as he banged her back out because it meant he was in the right place. Vyce was nothing without his stunts and shows. Everything he did had to be a performance or else he couldn't get his rocks off. He was all about power, and control.

Although Tya had dreams of reconciliation since the two parted on bad terms, Vyce was on some other shit at the moment. Tya betrayed him when she got into cahoots with Claire and Bobbi and it plagued his mind. Sure he wasn't fair for being with Bobbi, Claire and Tya at the same time. And sure he used Tya for her position at the real estate company she use to work for, which allowed him to place homes in both Claire and Bobbi's names. But in his mind Tya wasn't supposed to make a mental come up, and neither was Bobbi or Claire. The fact that they bonded together to get back at him made him feel as if his pimp game wasn't in tact. Tya, just like Claire and Bobbi, was supposed to play her position, which was under him at all times. So where did he go wrong?

Every time Vyce thought about how he rolled past the homes that he paid for, but put in the girls' names, only to realize that they short sold them and pocketed the money, he grew angrier. He wanted revenge but first he had to find Bobbi and Claire. Originally he felt the best way to them was Tya, but getting the information out of her was proving to be difficult.

The remaining Stick Up Kid he was about to kill for robbing him, who was in possession of Bobbi's wallet, said that Bobbi was no longer at Red's house in DC. Vyce had him on Red's place so that he could let him know the moment Bobbi showed her face again.

It got to the point where all of his thoughts were consumed with Claire and Bobbi, and he couldn't wait to get the revenge on them that he felt was necessary. And although immediate death would be sweet, he was

27

looking for a perfect plan. He wanted a way to destroy their lives, like they did his.

"Damn, my sweet baby, this pussy is so tight," Vyce complimented. "After all this time it feels like you ain't been with nobody else. I can tell. You still love me don't you?"

"Of course I do, Vyce," she said as she continued to fuck him hard. "I wanted you to see that I didn't fuck with another nigga the entire time we weren't together. 'Cause I don't care what happened between you, and me this pussy is still yours. And it's going to always be yours."

"You talking that good shit now," he said as he pawed her breasts. "You know what I like to hear don't you?"

"It's the truth, daddy, I never got over you and I never will."

Vyce bit down on his bottom lip, and pressed deeper into her body. Whenever one of his bitches begged him, it did nothing but send blood shooting straight to the tip of his dick. He lived for moments like that because it meant that he was in control. And if he didn't love anything else, he loved dominating the women he came in contact with along with breaking them down mentally.

"I'm about to cum, my sweet baby," he said. "Keep working those hips just like that. Don't change a thing."

When he said he was about to ejaculate, Tya hopped up like his dick was on fire. She positioned her head over his stick and went down to take him fully into her mouth. This was something she never did before, because she hated giving blowjobs or using her mouth for sexual pleasure.

"Damn, Tya, you doing that shit ain't you?" he asked looking down at her. She was pulling out all of her tricks to get back into his good graces and he loved every minute of it too.

"I'll do anything you want to win you back over," she said, speaking over his stiff dick as if it were a microphone. "And I do mean anything, Vyce."

I bet you would you dumb bitch. He thought to himself. *Before it's all said and done you will pay for your disloyalty. And you won't see it coming either.*

Vyce pressed down on her head and pushed into her mouth. When he felt the heat of her tongue trace over the tip of his dick he exploded into her throat. Tya tried to pop her head up like she always did when she was afraid she was about to choke but he wasn't having it.

"Swallow," he demanded. "You owe me this and you better not come up until you swallow every last drop."

Her eyes opened. "But…I…might get sick," she responded with a mouth full of dick. "I don't want to throw up."

"I don't give a fuck about you getting sick, Tya. You better be glad you're even in my presence considering what you did to me. Now drink my babies and get it all too. No let up."

Tya did what she was told and he didn't show his appreciation until her mouth opened wide and her tongue was clear. Only then did he allow her to crawl next to him on the bed, and place her head on his chest.

Since he was satisfied, Vyce rubbed her sweat-damped dreads and immediately got down to business. "Where are they, Tya? Where do Bobbi and Claire live?"

Tya's body seemed to stiffen. "I don't know, daddy."

"I don't believe you," he said plainly. "You were with them when they took my money and you said you went to their house before you caught a plane out of the state. So where are they now? I need an address."

Tya cleared her throat. "Vyce, I'm so serious. The last time I saw them they were in Delaware somewhere. And so much was going on that I didn't remember the address. All I wanted to do was get out of the area because I was afraid you would find them and kill me and my baby too."

"Isn't that convenient? That you don't remember anything right now?"

Tya's body trembled and she popped up, walked to the foot of the bed, dropped to her knees and got to massaging his feet. She knew every little thing that Vyce loved, and she worked overtime to prove to him that although she betrayed him, that she still knew how to please him too.

"Vyce, I promise you, I don't remember where they live," she said looking up into his eyes. "Like I said everything was happening so fast. I felt terrible that I betrayed you during that time, and I was just floating around the world with no existence"— she tugged on his big toe and it cracked— "when I got on the plane with the baby, I got so drunk I ended up throwing up. Somebody had to get my son for me because I couldn't even hold him. Everything after that was a blur."

He snatched his foot away and ran his toes over her bottom lip. "You're going to have to make it right, Tya"— He pushed her lip down so hard that her mouth opened— "I'm going to need you to make it real right." He stuffed three toes into her mouth and she ran her tongue between each toe.

"I'll do anything," she mumbled with her mouth full. "Anything at all."

"Good, because I'm sending you on a flight back to Delaware to find both of them bitches. And if you don't find out where they live, Tya, I'm going to show you what I originally had planned for your life, before I remembered how good that pussy was. Do you understand?"

She nodded and said, "Yes."

31

He smiled. "That's, my sweet baby. Now lick both of my feet clean."

CHAPTER 4

BOBBI

In Claire and Bobbi's living room in Delaware...

"I can't believe you coming at me like this, Claire," Bobbi yelled as she stood in front of the TV while Claire sat on the sofa. "You're not my mother you know? I am allowed to come and go as I please. Or is this prison or something?"

"Bobbi, it ain't about you coming and going as you please. It's about you respecting the fact that you in a relationship with me. You be gone so much that sometimes I forget you even live here."

Bobbi placed her hand over her heart just to be dramatic. "So I don't respect our relationship? Are you telling me that's how you feel? Do you really think that I don't appreciate and love you?"

"What the fuck do you think, Bobbi? You are never home and whenever you are, you either in the garage on the phone or downstairs in the basement trying to be slick. Talk to me, what's really going on?"

33

"I talk on the phone like that because I want some privacy sometimes, Claire. I am allowed you know?"

"Are you being faithful?"

"I hate this shit," she screamed. "You're treating me like a kid!"

"Why the fuck do you keep coming at me like that? Every time I ask you if you're being faithful, you give me all this other shit. At the end of the day the answer is either yes or no."

Bobbi walked into the kitchen and Claire followed her. "You know what, no matter what I say you're going to believe what you want anyway. It's a losing battle."

"Yes or no, Bobbi. It's as simple as that."

Bobbi opened the refrigerator, grabbed the jug of spring water and swallowed it from the spout. "I'm not even going to dignify that with a response. You go right ahead and believe what you choose."

"You are going to dignify the shit with a response or I'm done with you forever."

"Yeah right, like you could ever leave me," Bobbi said arrogantly.

"You really do believe that don't you? In your mind you are really cocky enough to believe that I won't dump you."

"Dump me," Bobbi giggled. "Picture that—"

"Were you with that nigga Red tonight?"

Bobbi almost choked on the water she was drinking. When she came home earlier today and Claire started grilling her about where she was, she never once thought she had actual facts. But here she was roll calling Red's name like their ordeal was on the news. Bobbi reasoned that if she knew that much, that she might know much more. So she had to change her game.

"I'm gonna keep it blunt with you. I was with Red but it wasn't even like that, trust me, Claire. I ran into him when I was out in the streets but we not messing around anymore."

Claire was visibly devastated. Her body seemed to deflate. "But what were you doing out D.C., Bobbi? You didn't even tell me you were going that far. What if something happened to you? I wouldn't even know where you were."

"Girl, bye, what the fuck going to happen to me in my hometown? My name rings in the streets and people know not to mess with me."

"Are you fucking serious? Vyce wants us dead! Have you forgotten already?"

"Claire, you acting as old as your name and for real, I'm getting tired of this shit. I feel like I'm Tristan in this house. Like I'ma child. I mean you need to back the fuck off with all this third degree nonsense. Just a little."

"You sure 'bout that? Are you certain that you want me to back off?"

"Yes, because I can't take it no more."

With her feelings hurt, Claire immediately turned around and hit it toward their bedroom. And in a change of events Bobbi was now on her heels.

"What are you about to do, Claire?" she asked looking over her shoulder.

Claire flipped on the lights to their room and rushed toward the closet. She grabbed a large Louis Vuitton suitcase, opened it, and flung it on the bed. Then she rushed over to the drawers and started pulling them open.

"Claire, what the fuck are you doing?" Bobbi repeated. She slammed one of the drawers shut while Claire was taking out her bras, and she almost smashed Claire's fingers in the process.

"If you want me out, I'll leave, Bobbi. I'm not about this life no more anyway so I'll step out of the way and let you do you."

"Claire, please don't do this shit. How come whenever you can't get your way, you want to bounce on me?"

Claire stopped in place. "Bitch, do you hear yourself right now?"

"Hold up," Bobbi frowned, ready to scratch her face up like she did people in her old Southeast D.C. days, "now I didn't come at you with disrespect, so don't come at me like that either. All I'm asking is why you call me out of my name when I didn't call you out of yours? That's wrong."

"I know what you're trying to do. You want to turn the tables around but I'm not with that game no more. Now if you want to be with the nigga Red, than you can do just that, but you won't have me too. Just as long as I can see Tristan I don't care what you do with your life." She stuffed her bras into the suitcase and went back to the drawer to grab her panties.

Bobbi's heart was beating rapidly because although she didn't want Claire, she didn't want to be alone either. "Claire, I am begging you not to do this. Just sit down for a minute and let's talk."

"You should be glad I'm leaving,"— Claire removed her panties from the drawer and stuffed them into the suitcase— "Now you don't have nobody telling you what to do and how to do it. You are free to flutter, little butterfly. So go, and do you."

Bobbi was feeling Claire in the traditional sense of the word, but the extra shit she did on a regular basis to get her way just rubbed Bobbi raw. Outside of the fact that Bobbi wasn't into the pussy bumping and eating coochie on a regular basis, she couldn't deal with the emotional side of dealing with women either. She preferred men because they weren't so bitchy, to hear Bobbi tell it.

"Claire, I wasn't going to tell you this because I knew you wouldn't understand, but I only saw Red to get some money. It's not like that between us no more you got to believe me. I really want to be with you, but

I hate that you always want to leave whenever we fight."

Claire stopped packing. "Fuck are you talking about to get some money? You should have at least a hundred grand in the bank if not more."

"I don't," she said honestly. "I would be surprised if I have a thousand."

"But why? We got Vyce for hundreds of thousands," she yelled. "What did you do?"

While Bobbi fixed her face to lie about how she ended up broke she knew the truth. Ever since Red found out that she came into a little cash, he sucked her harder than a plunger. Every week he called begging for money. First he said his car was broke and he needed three thousand for an engine. Then he told her he had to pay off his student loans, even though he didn't get past ninth grade in high school. At one point he even told her he had cancer in his balls, and he needed the money for a procedure, which cost twenty thousand dollars. Red wasn't doing anything but mooching off of Bobbi but she was so gone over the nigga's dick that she couldn't see over the tip of it.

"I had to pay my mother's taxes," Bobbi lied. "She needed most of my money so I gave it to her. That's why my bank is low."

Claire immediately felt bad. "Well how come you didn't ask me for the money?" Claire asked walking up to her. "I would've given it to you."

"Because you do so much for me already, and I love you," Bobbi said in a soft whisper. "I'm so sorry I lied about Red. Can we please start all over?"

When there was a knock at the door, Claire said, "Hold on, let me see who that is."

She walked toward the door and Bobbi followed. Bobbi was beside herself when she saw Natalie on the other side. Although Natalie never said it, Bobbi was aware that she didn't like her and the feeling was mutual. Bobbi saw herself in Natalie and she didn't like it one bit.

"Hey, Claire, what you doing?" Natalie asked. "I been beeping outside for about fifteen minutes. What's up we still going?"

"She's talking to her girlfriend, why don't you go on about your nosey business?" Bobbi suggested. "It's really not a good time."

Natalie smirked. "Listen little shawty doo, you may can talk fly to them other chicks on this block, but I'm a real bitch. Step back before I hurt your feelings and leave you in a box."

Bobbi was so angry she was ready to pull Natalie's bottom lip over top of her head. "You must want to get murdered coming in here talking like that to me. I don't know if you have amnesia or not, but this is my house."

Natalie just laughed her out and focused on Claire instead. "Are we going to the movies or what? I know they play previews for a long time, but if you wait any longer we're going to miss the movie too."

Claire looked back at Bobbi and decided that she didn't want to be around her. Besides, something in her heart told her that there was more going on with Red then she let on. "Yeah, I'm still rolling, let me grab my purse."

Bobbi couldn't believe Claire was about to leave while they were in mid conversation, because normally she'd be kissing her ass. "Claire, we were talking. The movies can wait."

"There's nothing else to talk about right now, Bobbi. Let's finish when I get back."

Natalie shook her head, laughed and said, "Claire, I'll be out in the car while you talk to your little girlfriend." She rolled her eyes at Bobbi and bounced off.

When Natalie was in her ride Bobbi said, "I don't want that bitch in my house again. I'm not fucking around with you. You can talk to her on the streets, but anybody threatening to put me in a box will find themselves missing."

"Bobbi, this is not just your house, it's mine too. Plus I don't feel like this shit right now." she grabbed her purse off of the counter.

"So in a middle of an argument you just bounce?"

"You've been out of the house all day while I've been in here with Tristan. Do yourself a favor. Be a mother for a minute, I'm out."

CHAPTER 5

In Ricky's kitchen in an upscale part of Maryland...

"...so I don't know what I should do, mommy," Claire said as she sat on the kitchen stool with Tristan in her lap. "I mean part of me believes she's not back with her ex-boyfriend, but I'm not sure, because why would she go to him for money and not tell me?"

Ricky sat on the stool across from her and tried her best to keep a straight face. The truth of the matter was she wasn't with all of the sudden dyking that her daughter was doing, but wanted to be there for her only child. Besides, the last time she got herself so worked up, she ended up hitting Claire, and they hadn't spoken until that moment.

"Well why the change all of a sudden, Claire? Bobbi has been going out for a while now and it never seemed to be a problem then. I mean if she told you she didn't do it, maybe you should just believe her." *Or dump the chick and find you a man.*

"Mommy, I know you're right and I'm so confused right now." The phone kept ringing off of the hook and Claire wondered why she didn't answer it. "And who is that blowing up your phone?"

42

"I'm not worried about all of that right now? I'm talking to my child."

"Like I was saying," she looked at her mother's ringing cell phone go off again. "I really do want to believe Bobbi, but part of me thinks—"

"Claire, why are you doing this?" Ricky interrupted. She seemed frustrated. "I gotta know. I can't take it anymore."

"Why am I doing what?" Claire played with the baby's fingers. When he started squirming around she sat him in the portable playpen at her feet. "What you talking about?"

"Why are you coming at me with all of this right now? Its one thing to ask me to respect your relationship with another woman, and now you're asking me to give you advice too? This is not me, Claire. You know how I feel about it and I think all you're doing is pushing me into a corner right now."

Claire frowned. "Mommy, I thought you said I could come at you about anything. And I definitely thought we were over the shit that happened at my house. I mean you are still one of the most important people in my life. I thought I could talk to you."

"And you can still talk to me, Claire. I just…I mean, this is a little more than I want to deal with."

"Why, ma?"

"For starters I want you to be in school, Claire." She responded in a caring tone. "I want you to get an education so that you can be set up for life. That was

43

always the dream I had for you. And right now I feel like the drama that this little girl is bringing upon your world is throwing you off. Not only that, what happened to the fact that a few years ago you were stomping this child out on the floor and trying to kill her? Remember that shit? Because you also dragged me in that shit too. That should be enough to show you what type of person you're dealing with. It's a reason you wanted to hurt her. She hasn't changed, Claire. You have."

Claire sighed. "Mommy, we been through all of this before. I was mad when I beat up Bobbi that night on the floor. She tried to drown me in a pool and I wanted to get her back. But we moved past that when we realized how much we had in common. People make mistakes you know?"

"Exactly," Ricky said shaking her head. "And they should be held accountable for them too. It seems to me like you forgave her without so much as the slightest bit of hesitation. And now you two are the best of friends? And lovers? It doesn't make any sense."

"But it's not for you to make sense of, ma. I told you what you needed to know about our relationship. It turns out that Vyce was the person involved in our problems. He was pitching me against her, and we were able to work on all of that because we love each other. The only thing I'm asking you to do is be a

44

mother to me, and not judge me so much. Can't you do that?"

"Claire, please," Ricky said hopping out of her seat. She walked over to the refrigerator just to get away. She wanted her daughter to see the error of her ways, but there was so much going on that she didn't know what she was angrier about. It was between her daughter dealing with another woman or the fact that she was not in school. "I don't want to hear about you being in love with no woman, Claire. I just don't. If you're asking me to be here for you, there has to be boundaries that you'll have to accept."

"But, mommy—"

"But mommy nothing"— she opened the refrigerator and grabbed herself a wine cooler— "I don't care what you say, I know you don't love that girl. You're just confused because of everything that has happened in your life. And at some point you're going to look back on this and realize you've made a great mistake."

"But I do love her…" she whispered.

"Even if that is true," she said after taking a sip of her drink. "What about the fact that this girl has no honor? Or no code? Huh? All she's going to do is break your heart, baby. Maybe if the girl was nicer…and she treated you right, I could see you being with her," she explained. "You have to understand that if you want me to be a proponent for your relationship that you have to give me something I can stand on. I don't see that right now."

Just the thought of her daughter eating another woman's pussy caused her stomach to squirm. But, if Bobbi was sweet she could see herself coming around.

"I'm starting to feel like I can't talk to you about anything, no matter what you tell me. And if that is the case, it bothers me a lot."

"Claire, don't be melodramatic."

"I'm serious, ma, if I can't talk to you, we don't have a bond anymore. And if we don't have a bond, we don't have a relationship." She looked into her mother's eyes. "Is that what you want?"

Ricky was about to address her daughter when her boyfriend Humphrey walked through the backdoor in the kitchen. Humphrey was forty-six years old, six foot four inches tall and had brown skin. But his face was littered with tiny black moles, he looked as if he had a hard life and was pushing sixty years old. No matter what the weather, he didn't leave out without his thick black leather vest.

Without even acknowledging Claire, he walked up to Ricky, planted a fat sloppy kiss on her lips and pulled her toward his body. He gripped her thick butt cheeks, squeezed and slithered his fingers into the crack of her ass.

"Hump," Ricky laughed, wiggling out of his hold before slapping his hands. "You see my daughter over there. You giving her too much for this early in the day."

"Oh, hey, Claire," he grinned before pinching Ricky's nipple. "I'm being rude and shit. Didn't even see you."

Claire didn't respond. She rolled her eyes.

"You are a mess today," Ricky declared, trying not to blush so hard at his aggressive affections. She hadn't had a man since two-dollar bills were in rotation so she was beside herself with giddiness. "What you been doing...drinking? You smell like you been bathing in the bottle all day."

"I been thinking about your fine ass and wondering why you ain't been answering the phone. You got me thinking somebody was in that sweet hairy pussy I love so much of yours."

"Hump, my daughter," she yelled trying to remind him of Claire's presence. "Not so vulgar please."

"My bad."

"And I'm sorry I didn't answer the phone, I just been talking to my baby that's all."

He looked at Claire and said, "Well I hope ya'll wasn't talking about that dyke she be rolling with again. She talking to you about that shit so much she making me think she wants to convert you too."

Claire's eyes spread wide, because she couldn't believe his comment. Not only was he out of pocket for even coming at her like that, but the fact that her mother shared her business with him infuriated her. I

47

mean who was he to say shit about anybody else, when his shoes were run over and the stains on the white t-shirt he sported had matching yellow sweat spots?

"What the fuck you talking about," Claire bucked on him. "You don't know shit about me or who I be with. You better care for how you look when you come out of the house before you try schooling me on anything."

He frowned, and gave her a look to kill. "I know what your mother told me about your relationship and how the girl doesn't respect you, and if you ask me that's enough. You too young to be moving the way that you are. That's all I'm saying."

"And that makes you some kind of judge? Or jury?"

"No but it makes—"

"Humphrey, please don't do this right now," Ricky said softly. "Leave her alone." When he didn't appear to be calming down she rubbed both sides of his face. "Please, baby. I haven't seen her since our last argument and I wanted today to be smooth."

Humphrey took one last look at Claire and focused on his lady. "My bad, sweetheart. Just didn't want you having to deal with your problems all alone. Especially since you got me to bear some of the weight on your shoulders. So if I spoke out of turn I apologize."

"I know you worry about me, honey, " Ricky said kissing his dry lips. "And it's over and done with.

Now what you doing over here so early? I didn't expect to see you until later on tonight."

"I was coming to see if my sweetie could loan me a few bucks until payday. You know I hate to do you like this but it's an emergency. So what do you say? Can you help a nigga out or what?"

"You can't be serious," Claire interrupted shaking her head. "You got something smart to say out of your mouth to me and you broke? You are a fucking joke!" she laughed.

"Claire," Ricky yelled. "Please don't talk like that."

Claire shook her head and remained quiet. But she definitely knew what kind of bum her mother was dealing with now. A no good ass one.

"How much you need baby?" Ricky asked him.

He rolled his eyes at Claire and focused on Ricky. "A hundred will get me right until payday"—he kissed Ricky on the neck and tiny goosebumps popped up all over Ricky's skin— "the money is on its way. I just don't have access to it right now. But the moment I get paid I'll hook you up too."

"Sure, baby," Ricky said. "I know you good for it"

She walked away from him, and over to the drawer next to the refrigerator where she kept all of her short money. She pulled out the envelope and removed two crisp one hundred dollar bills.

49

"Here you go," she handed it to him. "Give it back if you can."

He grinned wider than a hula-hoop as he stuffed the money in his back pocket. He slobbed her down and then stuffed his tongue into her mouth. "I appreciate this. You always did know how to take care of me." He slapped her ass so hard that the sound was still there long after he was gone.

After he left Claire asked, "Mommy, why would you give him money? He's supposed to be taking care of you."

"We have an understanding, Claire. Instead of worrying about me and mines, you should be worrying about yours. I'm not the one over here asking for advice, you are."

When Ricky walked out of the kitchen Claire's phone rang. Her heart dropped when she heard Bobbi's frantic voice on the line. "What's wrong, baby."

"Claire, that bitch Natalie called this house. I'm going to kill her. I swear to God!"

CHAPTER 6

VYCE

In V yce's bedroom in G eorgetown W ashington D C ...

Vyce was on his bed with an eighteen-year old Mel under his body. Her cousin, twenty-year-old Juniper was behind him, stuffing her tongue within the walls of his asshole. If Vyce was known for anything, it was keeping a young girl under him at all times. The need to control someone else, since he couldn't control himself, stayed with him always.

How he met them was quite regular. Vyce was pushing his silver Maserati down the street when he happened upon a small brick house on East Capitol St in southeast Washington D.C. And to his surprise four girls, who called themselves The Lollipop Kidz, stood in the middle of the street twerking in front of his car. Twerking was the act of bouncing one's ass up and down with precise motions and the Lollipop Kidz were the All Stars.

Vyce's dick immediately stiffened as he watched Mel, the lighter one out of the bunch, twerk so hard, the pink and white flower dress she wore rose up and revealed her white cotton panties and yellow ass cheeks underneath. She did all of this with a huge smile on her face.

Just when he was about to step out of his car and pronounce her queen, her cousin Juniper, who had skin as smooth as a dark brown crayon, strutted into the middle of the street and twerked next to her. She was just as beautiful. Her ass cheeks seemed to suck in the tight red shorts she was wearing, causing them to virtually disappear before his eyes.

He not only wanted them, he had to have them that day. Not wasting time Vyce parked his car in the middle of the street, and the other member of The Lollipop Kidz got out and approached his beautiful ride. Juniper and Mel stopped what they were doing and eye fucked him and his car. Both girls were still young so they dated cars on a regular. Which was to say their loyalty to a man depended upon what he was driving, not on how he treated them. So to them, at the moment, Vyce Anderson was king.

"That's your car," Mel said, sucking her bottom lip as she looked up into his eyes. "Cause if it is, it's real nice. My brother had one like this before he went to college, but I think he sold it to buy books."

Vyce laughed at her naivety. "If your brother had a car like this and sold it, he would've gotten way more paper than enough for some books."

"Oh, well I think you look good as shit driving in it anyway." She ran her finger along the side of the car. "Real nice."

"What you think?" He asked looking at Juniper. "You like my car as much as she does?" He nodded toward Mel.

He could smell the salty sweat from their skin and loved every bit of it. Vyce felt as if he was the one man on planet earth who appreciated the natural musty odor of a woman's pussy.

"I think I want to fuck you inside your car," Juniper responded, licking her lips. "That's what I think. So what you think about that?"

Vyce laughed, appreciating the girl's forwardness. And as he looked at the other member of the Lollipop Kidz, he was already in full plot mode. They were equally as cute and he felt like he was a kid in the candy store. He was greedy when it came to his ambition for women. He felt he was well within his rights to have two or more at the same time, and since most women he came into contact with never stopped him, or put him in his place, he continuously tried his hand.

"What's your name, my sweet baby?" he asked the light skin one first. "You were looking kind of good in the middle of the street doing your thang, and I like what I see."

"They call me Mel Boo Boo, but you can call me Mel," she winked. "If you take care of me, you can call me anything you want."

53

He smirked. "Is that right?"

"It sure is," she grinned.

"And you?" he asked the darker and equally pretty one.

"I'm Juniper," she said seductively. "And you can call me tonight if you want too."

He had to give one thing to the girls. And that was that they were forward and straight up, and in a world where everybody beat around the bush he appreciated that. The Lollipop Kidz didn't have access to YMCA's, or after school programs. So they turned to the one thing that was always there for them, the streets and because of it they were always in danger.

"Look, I'm going to be real with both of you. I want to fuck you both. As a matter of fact, I'm trying to get with all of you." He looked at the other one and she grinned at him. He focused back on Mel and Juniper. "Now if you can get with that climb in the back seat of my car and I'll show you the world…my world. If not, I don't have nothing for you."

The moment his lips closed Mel and Juniper were pulling at the handle of his car door. That was two weeks ago, and they had been fucking ever since. Although he hadn't worked on the other one just yet, he penciled her in his schedule for later that week. He was confident that it wouldn't be a problem because the world belonged to him, to hear him say it.

After he bent them over properly, he took them on a shopping spree at Rainbow clothing store. He watched as they snatched hoochie outfit after hoochie outfit and had the sales girl, "Put it in the Bag". Vyce laughed to himself because you would've thought they were in Bloomingdales the way they were carrying on. All they kept saying was how everything was so cute and hot.

When they were done, they had so many clothes on the counter; it took two cashiers to get their purchases together. Over and over they kept thanking their daddy for what he did for him. And when they were done ringing up the purchases, everything came too only three hundred twenty. Vyce texted his boys because he thought it was hilarious how cheap they sold themselves to him.

After the shopping spree, he got a call from Diane saying she needed a little financial help. She was Whiz's, his homie who was murdered, baby's mother. When Whiz was killed Vyce stepped up and became a father figure for both of Whiz's baby's mothers. This despite having Tya believe that he wasn't the father of her baby. He did a much better job of *pretending* to be a good father than he did at actually being one.

"Where we going," Juniper asked who was sitting in the front seat of his car. "We been driving for twenty minutes and I thought we were going to get something to eat and then go back to your house to play around a little." She was sucking a purple lollipop (hence the name The Lollipop Kidz), which left a purple trail on her tongue leading toward her throat.

"Yeah, I thought you were treating us to IHOP for pancakes," Mel said in the back seat. Her legs were gaped open, revealing her red panties. "We ain't eat all day."

"Fall back," Vyce told both of them sternly. "Anyway you go where the fuck I tell you you're going remember?"— He looked at both of them, revealing a glimpse of the killer he could be — "Am I clear, or do I have to get a little louder and harder?"

"Y-yes, you're clear," Juniper stuttered hoping he wouldn't cut her off of his blessings for her insolence. "I was just asking. It's your world, Vyce."

Lately he allowed the girls to think they were running things, but it was all a part of his game. He loved getting young girls wrapped up so that when he was ready, he could fuck their minds up, and have them thinking that they did something to cause the shift in his personality when it really was his plan all along.

Vyce parked his car in front of Diane's beautiful brick house in Maryland, and walked to the house. The moment she opened the door he was reminded why Whiz chose her. Although Whiz was white, he loved black women and picked a winner when it came to Diane. She was tall, about 5'10, with a smooth brown complexion that always made her look bronzed. She was wearing a purple maxi dress that showed off her fat breasts and curvy hips, and the way she stood in the doorway let the world know that she was confident.

"Hey, Vyce," she said hugging him. "Thanks for coming over. I know it's nice outside, and you wanted to enjoy the weather so I appreciate you stopping by."

"Not a problem, sexy," he said licking his lips. "But how is that pussy…I mean…Noodles doing?" Noodles was her daughter.

She giggled. "You better stop talking like that out loud, nigga. If my daughter knew her uncle Vyce was tapping into these goods she would be devastated. Even with Whiz gone you know she can't see past her father."

"Well I guess we better never let her find out then." He winked and dug into his pocket and pulled out a stack. "Here's the money I was going to give you. I'll stop by later and give you some more when I catch my other I just—"

His sentence was cut off when he heard glass break. When he turned in the direction of the noise, he saw Mel and Juniper with no shoes on crashing Diane's car window in her driveway. Slivers of glass covered the streets and landed in small piles.

"What the fuck," Diane screamed pushing past Vyce, who was right behind her. "Who the fuck are these bitches? And why are they fucking with my car?"

Vyce rushed over to Mel and snatched the bat out of her hand. She was wearing a pair of gloves he guessed to get away with the crime. He grabbed her by the forearm. "What the fuck is wrong with ya'll?"

"Who is that bitch, Vyce?" Mel asked, snatching away from him. "You fucking around on us? After everything we been through? You just bought us some clothes and everything!"

This boggled his mind because he just met them. "Am I fucking around on ya'll, are you fucking crazy, bitch?" he yelled. "How the fuck am I fucking over on somebody who I ain't even with? Explain that to me?"

"No, you the one who crazy," Juniper added. "You might be telling us that you not fucking with us now, but that wasn't what you were saying earlier tonight when you stuffed your dick in each of our holes. Now who the fuck is she?"

Before he could respond, the cops were speeding down the block toward them. One of Diane's neighbors saw them destroying her car, and made the call. The cops parked their cars in front of Diane's house and immediately assessed the situation. It wasn't hard to point a finger at the troublemakers. Not even five minutes later, Juniper and Mel were thrown in the back of the police cruiser where their twerking days would be stopped momentarily while they were hauled off to jail.

Afterwards Vyce paid Diane to get her car fixed, and fucked her long and hard for her troubles. He started to go home, but suddenly he had an idea. Females that ghetto and bold had to be good for something, and he knew just what.

CHAPTER 7

BOBBI

M eanwhile in a black M ercedes B enz...

"I don't know about you anymore, Red," Bobbi said as she steered angrily down the street on the way home while talking to him on the phone. "You played me worse than anybody ever has in my life. And I'm not sure if I can trust you anymore."

"I know I fucked up, but I feel like if I didn't tell him you had the money he would've killed us both. Think about it for a second, baby. The niggas had guns to our heads. I mean don't you think it's a little selfish to get mad at me for telling him about the few bucks you had in your purse? I was trying to save our lives."

"That's some bullshit," she said pulling over in front of a run down liquor store. "You could've done something else, Red, anything but put me out there. I mean how do I know it wasn't a set up."

"You can't be serious," he said seriously. "On my mother's new heart I didn't know nothing about that shit."

She was about twenty minutes from home and wanted to drag the phone call out for as long as possible. Besides, once she was in the house Claire would be all up in her business and she didn't feel like dealing with her right now. Being home was bad for her privacy, and it was also annoying because Claire was around her twenty-four seven.

Speaking to Red on the phone, even if he was no good, was relaxing, and she lived for those moments. Just the sound of his voice did something to her physically. Besides, after hearing from her cousin that Vyce was asking around her old neighborhood in Washington D.C. about her, she wanted to do something that made her feel good and sadly enough he was it.

"Like I said, that's bullshit, Red," she said. "Come better."

"What do you mean it's some bullshit, Bobbi? I'm serious, and I would never play with you like that. I have my shit with me but I would never turn against you in that way. I know it's terrible that you got, got for your dough but look at it on the good side."

"And what's that?" she said pressing the phone against her ear.

"If you didn't have the money in your purse they may have killed us."

"You said that already, Red, and it doesn't make me feel any better."

"Is that why you haven't been answering my phone calls? Because you mad at me for something I had no control over?"

"What do you think?" She frowned, as she also tried to think of an excuse on why the pizza would be cold once she made it home. "If everything was sweet we wouldn't have beef but you and I both know that this is not the case. You stabbed me in the back."

"Let me make it up to you, Bobbi," he begged. "Just give me one more chance to show you I can be the nigga you love. And if you don't want to fuck with me after that, I'll let you go."

She ran her fingers over the fibers of the leather steering wheel. "How do you intend on making it up to me this time?"

He chuckled in a way that let her know that he knew how to get back in. "I got something that's going to toss your head around."

"And what's that?"

"I'm in Delaware right now. Looking for you."

Her heartbeat stammered. "What...I mean...why?"

"Because I can't stand what's happening between us, baby girl," he said in a deep throaty voice. "And since you ain't fucking with D.C. no more, I decided to fuck with you instead out here. So let me come see you so that we can talk this shit out like we grown instead of kids. Please, Bobbi."

Bobbi thought about what it would mean to say yes. If she met up with him she could pretty much forget about having a serious relationship with Claire. Although Claire was crazy about her, it was obvious

61

that she was done with the games she was playing too. Saying yes to him may have been simple to him but to her it could fuck up everything, including her long-term relationship.

"I can meet you for fifteen minutes, but after that I got to go home. So if you try to spend any more time with me you gonna be on your own."

Not even ten minutes later Bobbi's Benz was parked behind the liquor store instead of the front. She was in the back getting her sugar walls pounded, and her toes were curled up in the tennis shoes on her feet. Red was stuffing her so well that she felt like the tip of his dick would pop out of the bottom of her stomach. He always knew how to take care of her and this time was no exception.

"Damn this pussy is wet," Red said looking down at her sweaty back. "Keep backing that thing up, baby girl. I'm almost there."

Bobbi twisted and pushed into him so hard that not even forty seconds later he ejaculated inside of her body. This wasn't the first time he'd done this and it wouldn't be the last if she had anything to do with it. She could care less that she was going home to Claire, with whom she shared an oral relationship. She was all about self.

When he was done, he fell into her back and breathed heavily into her nape. "I fucking love you girl," he said rising up to pull his dick out of her body. A drop of his cum fell onto her car seat, and he left it there hoping that Claire would find it. "Did you hear what I said? I love you."

"I hope you mean it, Red," she said crawling into the front seat, behind the steering wheel. It was difficult because her jeans hung at her thighs. "I been in love with you for a long time." She pulled her jeans up.

Red stayed in the back and looked up at her. "I do mean it but I'm also getting tired of hooking up with you just to fuck. I want something more, Bobbi. I want a full time relationship and the last I heard; I thought you wanted it too. Are you changing your mind on me?"

Bobbi sighed. "I'm not changing my mind but you know I can't do that right now, Red. If I could I would. But my situation is all tossed up. I been told you that."

"So let me get this straight, one minute you love me and the next you don't? What about the business we were going to open up together? It's sad that you letting this bitch come in the way of us making money."

Bobbi frowned and looked back at him. "By getting money together are you referring to the barbershop that I funded all by myself, that won't even have my name on it?" she asked sarcastically.

"Bobbi, I been told you the reason I need to put the business in just my name. You got good credit but I don't. Having this business in my name would set me up good and allow me to be able to put my name on the house too that we talked about. It ain't that I don't want your name on it, you know that. It's still both of our business."

Bobbi didn't believe him but she couldn't let him go either. "I can't leave Claire right now, Red. I just can't. But when the time is right I will and you're going to have to trust me."

Red was beyond frustrated. Truthfully he could care less what she did with her time. It was her money he was in love with. Although Bobbi's pussy was top notch, and at one time he wanted to be with her, it soon became evident that she wasn't the marrying type. She had a foul mouth, roamed through his shit when he wasn't looking, and never gave him space. On an average day he wanted nothing to do with her unless it involved her dough.

But the moment he broke up with her back in the day, after catching her going through his shit, he became aware that she was fucking with Vyce, a romantic drug dealer with money to spare. So he dug his fingers back into her heart until he was right where he wanted to be, in her bank account. But there was one thing holding him back, and it was Bobbi's girlfriend Claire. He was going to have to work overtime if he was going to get Claire out of the picture, and get that barbershop by next year.

"What is it about her?" he asked. "That you love so much?"

"She's a nice person whose only crime was running into me," she said honestly. "I guess I'm a monster."

Mad at her response, he scooped his nut up, opened the box of pizza that sat on the back seat and smeared it on one of the pepperoni. He laughed at himself for what he'd just done. It was both gross and unnecessary just like his presence.

"You know she's a good person right?" Bobbi said to him. "She is really sweet. It's just that I don't look at her in the way that she wants me to."

"Why you telling me this shit?" he asked, easing into the front seat.

"Because I want you to know if it wasn't for that, maybe things wouldn't be so hard, and I could be with you."

"Who the fuck you fooling, Bobbi?" he laughed. "I know what the real situation is and it has nothing to do with her being a good person. The girl takes care of the kid and you like it because you don't—"

She frowned. "His name is Tristan and he's your son," she reminded him, looking over at him. "He's not just some kid."

"That's what you said, but how can I be sure he's mine?"

"You can be sure because we took the test remember? And the test said that you are 99.9% the father. So unless you got a twin brother around here with the same DNA as you that I don't know about, I'd say that you're the father."

"There's always the one percent, and you need to know that I don't have no money, Bobbi." He went totally left field, always afraid that someone was going to take him to court for child support.

"I know that, Red," she said rolling her eyes. "But I am serious about you being the father," she frowned.

"And I'm serious too. It wasn't like you wasn't flaunting that pussy around the entire Southside about two years ago, telling everybody who could sit down how you were pregnant by drug kingpin Vyce Anderson. And now all of a sudden you want me to believe the kid is mine? You gotta forgive me if I feel like things are a little shifty."

"You don't have to believe shit," she yelled trying to prevent herself from crying. "Let the paternity test speak for itself, because it said you are the father."

He shrugged. "Anyway it don't even matter." He sat back in the seat and looked out ahead of him. He was trying to ruffle the hairs on her body and it was working. "The baby ain't yours or mine."

"How you sound?"

Red shook his head. "Where is the baby now, Bobbi?" he paused. "With Claire right?" he paused again looking into her eyes. "And where was the baby yesterday?" he paused. "With Claire right? Before long you not going to have to worry about being a mother, or me being a father because she's going to take him away from you."

"That shit ain't happening." She shook her head from left to right rapidly. "I ain't hardly worried about all of that."

Although Bobbi was shaking her head, she was heated knowing that what he was saying was part true. Tristan only cried when Claire left the room. He could care less when Bobbi left or more importantly when she would be coming back. Just thinking about how baby Tristan turned his back on her made her so hot that you could fry eggs on her thighs if you had a mind to.

Bobbi was just getting ready to put Red out of her car when through her rearview mirror she saw a dude sitting in a black Caprice. She'd seen that same guy in that same car not even two days ago and she didn't like how he made her feel. Scared.

Bobbi knew what was happening now. She was being followed.

CHAPTER 8

CLAIRE

In Claire and Bobbi's living room...

Claire paced the floor as she spoke to Bobbi on the phone. The moment Claire heard her voice she knew something was wrong. It took everything in her power not to be as frantic as she was, but she knew if she was hysterical too that it wouldn't help. "Calm down, baby, because I don't want you driving while you're like that. If you don't chill out you're going to get into an accident."

Claire was beside herself with worry. One moment she was putting Tristan to bed and the next minute she was getting a call from her frantic girlfriend.

"It's hard to calm down right now, Claire, you not the one who got some crazy ass nigga chasing you. I could be shot, or ran off the side of the road. This shit serious."

Claire sat down on the sofa, knowing that Bobbi was right. Her left leg shook rapidly as she did the only thing she could do, wait. Claire always felt like when she murdered Whiz, Vyce's best friend, that it would come back to haunt her and she figured now

68

was the time. Bobbi would pay for her sins and it was all Claire's fault.

A couple of years ago when Claire and Bobbi made a decision to be together, Whiz was on to them and their plans to rob Vyce. And to prevent him from telling Vyce what they were up to, Claire took his life.

Although Bobbi pretty much moved on and gave little thought to the murder, taking another person's life always bothered Claire. Not only because she never killed anybody before, but she believed heavily in karma. She knew that in some way, on some day, God would be coming back to make good on what she'd done. The only question was when.

"Bobbi, you right, and I'm so sorry," Claire looked down at her hands and tried to relax her mind and heart. "Just drive slowly so you won't get into an accident. Is he still behind you?"

There was a slight pause. "I don't see him anymore." Bobbi exhaled deeply and said, "But while you're on the phone, can I ask you something?"

"You can ask me anything," she said walking over to the bar to pour herself a glass of Red Berry Ciroc. "What's up?"

"Are you still mad at me?"

"Bobbi, I'm not mad at you anymore," she said sipping her liquor. "I just need a little more from you in this relationship that's all. I mean, if you are going to be with me, I need you to fully commit without the games."

69

"I am fully committed," she lied "It's just that, I mean, I wish you would allow me to experience other things too that's all. I feel like what we got going on can really work if we didn't have so many boundaries."

Claire sat the drink on the bar. Not this shit again. "Fuck are you talking about now?"

"It's like this, I know I love you and you know you love me. But, this is the first time I ever been in a relationship like this before, Claire. I mean with another woman and all, and sometimes I think I jumped in too quickly."

Claire sighed having heard all of this before. She grabbed her glass of vodka and walked back over to the sofa to wait. "What exactly are you asking me, Bobbi? Because you brought this up before but you never elaborated."

"Would you have a problem with me experiencing men one last time? Just so I can make sure that it's out of my system?"

Claire almost choked on her drink. She sat it down on the floor to focus on the call instead. "Bobbi, were you ever really being followed?"

"What? Of course I was," she yelled. "Why would you even ask me that shit?"

"So you're being followed, and the only thing you can think about right now is fucking another nigga?" Claire paused. "Because let's be clear, if I even think you're fucking around on me it's over."

"So you are saying you would have a problem with me experiencing men again?" she said in a frustrated tone. "You know what, don't even answer that now, I'm out front. I'll talk to you in a minute."

Before she could respond Claire saw the lights from Bobbi's car pull up in the driveway. She hung the phone up, and walked over to the door to open it for her. Bobbi was holding the pizza that they were supposed to share for dinner two hours ago.

"Are you still being followed?" Claire asked before they got into their conversation, and what she really wanted to know.

"I was able to shake them but I know the nigga was with Vyce," Bobbi said as she tossed her purse on the sofa along with the cold pizza. "I seen him before when I was at the grocery store." She grabbed the vodka on the floor and downed it. "He was just watching me, and not saying anything."

"Where were you when they were following you?" Claire asked, trying to figure out what was going on.

"Not this shit again, Claire," she sighed.

"Bitch, you better tell me something I want to hear," Claire yelled. "I'm tired of every time I ask you a question it's a fucking problem. Where were you when them niggas rolled up on you?"

"I was getting the pizza, Claire," she said pointing at it. "Did you forget about that while you were too busy asking me about where I was?"

Claire was growing weary with Bobbi and her bullshit, and she wasn't attracted to her in the same way. It was as if Bobbi was working overtime just to be trifling. "You know what, I don't even care where you were anymore. Earlier today you were asking me about men. So is that what you want to do? Deal with dudes on the side."

"It's not about dudes."

"Then what is it?"

Bobbi sighed. "You want to know what the ideal situation would be for me?"

"Do tell, Bobbi Bonds Gannon."

"In that case I will," she said crossing her legs. "The ideal situation for me would be if I could be in a relationship with you, that's loving and strong, but then I'll also have somebody else on the side too."

Claire was so angry her hair was shivering. For a brief moment she considered what it would be like to strangle her. When she realized that if she were locked up Bobbi would really be able to do what she wanted, she decided against it. This entire relationship with Bobbi was turning out to be a big mistake. Her mother and Natalie were right.

"Let me make something clear to you, Bobbi, because after I say this I don't want no misunderstanding"— she stepped up to the couch— "if dick comes anywhere near your pussy, your pussy won't be coming anywhere near me."

"I can't believe you're acting like this. I mean, I thought we could talk about anything, Claire."

"You know the saddest part about all of this shit, you don't see anything wrong with how you coming at me. I mean, did I make you think things would ever be that cool with us? That you could come at me like that and I would just accept it? Do you think I'm that weak?"

"It's not about that, Claire, I just want to be able to talk to you about how I'm feeling. So that you'll know where I'm coming from."

"And you can talk to me about anything," she said, "and I'm allowed to talk to you about anything too. I'm not a pushover, Bobbi, and I hope that you forgive me if I gave you the wrong impression. Nobody is ever walking over me again, and that means you too."

When the baby started crying Claire left Bobbi like she wasn't even a factor, to see about Tristan instead. Claire walked into the baby's room and Bobbi was right behind her. "Let me get him, Claire."

Claire backed up and allowed her to hold her own child. But the moment she put her hands on Tristan's underarms to lift him up out of the bed, he cried louder. It was as if she was pinching him the way he was carrying on. Not only did he cry hysterically in Bobbi's face, he took to pooping in his pamper too. He did not want her anywhere near him despite her being his mother.

Bobbi never gave any consideration to the bond she was throwing away with her son for the love of Red and the streets. She took for granted that just because she popped him out of her pussy, that he would love her automatically. She never thought that he would love Claire or anyone else for that matter, more than he loved her, and she was wrong.

"Why are you crying," Bobbi said, trying to rock him in her arms. His body stiffened with her touch. "It's mommy, nigga, don't cry, I'm here now. I got you."

Tristan wasn't trying to hear anything she was saying. He wanted her hands off of him and he wanted her hands off of him immediately.

Claire couldn't take it anymore. She hated to see him suffer because she loved him like a mother to her only son. "Let me hold him, Bobbi. He probably has to have his pamper changed or something."

Instead of giving him to her she twisted her body to hold him out of her reach. "Well I can do it you know? I'm not dumb."

Despite how she felt, Claire allowed Bobbi to do her thing, even though Tristan's screams were breaking her heart.

Bobbi walked Tristan over to the changing table as he continued to scream his lungs out. While Bobbi removed his pamper, Tristan was determined not to calm down. It was then that Claire realized that she couldn't take it anymore and needed to help Bobbi.

"I got him, Bobbi," Claire said coming to the rescue. Her voice was real calm. "Go into the living room and relax. You had a long day."

"I guess you right," Bobbi said looking down at Tristan. "When you done with him just come back into the living room with me so we can finish our conversation."

Immediately, the moment Claire laid her hands on his legs, he not only stopped crying, but he also took to smiling and laughing. Bobbi watched on in jealousy at how Bobbi cleaned him up, kissed his little feet and played with his fingers.

Claire had no idea how angry Bobbi was, until she slapped Tristan in the face.

CHAPTER 9

VYCE

In Mama's Kitchen restaurant in Washington D.C ...

Vyce was inside of a popular restaurant with Mel and Juniper. Ever since he bonded them out of jail, they were at his beckon call. If they weren't massaging his feet, they were cooking and cleaning his house as if they were slaves. In a way it reminded him of when Bobbi and Claire were under his spell, minus the drama. Mel and Juniper knew each other first and got along, so in his mind this situation was foolproof.

When they were especially good, on the nights they would perform their sex routine so well that it would cause his toes to curl, he would take them shopping at their favorite hood rat spots. The girls were open and now it was time to kick things up another notch. It was time to get them to do what he wanted them to do.

Vyce took his phone out of his pocket and sat it on the table, while Mel and Juniper dug into their meals. "Everything good?" He asked them. From the corner of his eyes he looked at the phone as he waited on it to ring.

"How about we show you how good the food is when we leave here," Juniper said, tearing off a piece of biscuit before stuffing it into her warm mouth. "You always take care of us and now we want to take care of you."

"You know I can't wait to see that shit too," he chuckled.

"She not lying," Mel added. "We been practicing this routine that we saw on the porn channel the other day. And now it's time to see if it works."

"And what's that?" he said.

"We both put our legs behind our heads and sit our pussies on top of each other's. Our assholes stay out so you can hit them as you please."

"Ya'll some freaky little bitches," he thought.

"You know it," Juniper added kissing Mel.

While Vyce nursed his drink, he looked at his phone again. He was waiting on the person who was supposed to call him, so that he could enact his plan. But since the nigga was late he was about to fake a silent call and proceed with his plan. But five minutes later, his phone rung and vibrated on the menu on the table.

"Give me a second, babies," he said holding his finger up. Vyce picked up the phone and said, "Who this? I'm busy right now."

"Sorry I'm late man," Butch said on the other line. *"My girl was—"*

"What you talking about?" Vyce said loudly. He paused for effect. "Yeah I know them, they my babies why?" He rubbed the top of Juniper's hand softly, letting it be known that the conversation was about them.

Although Butch had no idea what was going on, it didn't matter to Vyce. Vyce just needed the call to come through so that he could pretend that Butch was saying things that he wasn't.

"Am I supposed to say something?" Butch asked, trying to figure out what Vyce was talking about. *"I'm confused."*

Vyce continued to talk over him, never answering one of his questions. At the moment Butch was as useless as a used tampon. "Aight, cuz, I'ma call you back to ask them about that shit, because something sounds off to me. But if it's true I'm gonna go off in this bitch." He ended the call in still dumbfounded Butch's ear.

Vyce turned off his smooth attitude and replaced it with one that was filled with rage when he addressed the girls. "I gotta talk to ya'll about something and I don't want no games either."

"What's wrong, baby?" Mel asked, scared out of her mind. "Is everything okay?"

"Yeah, did we do something wrong?" Juniper added.

"I'm going to ask ya'll one time and you better kick it to me straight too." He kept looking left and right between them. "Do either one of you bitches got HIV?"

Mel almost threw up on the table. Although her aunt Mark had HIV, as far as she knew, she was clean.

Even Juniper's knees knocked against one another while she tried to figure out what was going on. Although she didn't know her health status, she heard that people with HIV looked skinny and sick, and she was neither. So that meant she was fine right?

Both girls knew nothing about STD's nor did they care about what could possibly happen to their bodies while they were out fucking the world. As a matter of fact, both of them possessed fresh cases of Chlamydia at the moment, and instead of going to a doctor, they opted to let the symptoms go away on their own. And as a result, Vyce, Juniper and Mel passed it back and forth to each other, and they didn't even know it.

"Vyce, I don't know who you talked to, but somebody lied to you. I don't have no mothafucking HIV," Juniper proclaimed. "I mean look at me." She raised her arms. "Do I look sick to you?"

"I'm with Jun," Mel added. "We don't got none of that shit."

"Well that ain't what the streets is saying," Vyce said cracking his knuckles. "If ya'll gave me that shit

79

it's going to be straight murder was the case out here. And I'm talking to both of you too."

"Who out here saying that shit?" Mel asked, rage painted all over her face. "Can you at least tell us that?"

"Two bitches named Bobbi and Claire. They heard I was fucking with ya'll and they got word back to me through one of my friends."

"You talking about southeast Bobbi Bonds Gannon?" Mel asked with her jaw dropped. "The one who use to fuck with the boy Red from Northwest?"

"Yeah, her."

"I swear on my life, on my baby's life and on my dying gay uncle that I don't have no HIV," Mel said. She was prepared to swear on her entire family if it would've made a difference. "Them bitches lied because they jealous, and they want to tear us apart."

"Yeah, you know how females are," Juniper added trying hard not to cry.

Vyce stood up and walked out. "Where you going?" Mel asked already crying hysterically. Suddenly the food made her stomach spin and she felt sick. If she lost that nigga she was going to kirk out on somebody, anybody.

"I'm getting away from you two sluts," he said to them evilly. "Find a way to pay the check yourself. I'm out of here."

He dipped into his car, laughing the entire way.

CHAPTER 10

BOBBI

T he next day in B obbi's car...

"Pookie, you don't understand what the fuck I went through last night. I mean this bitch actually had the nerve to put her hands on me," Bobbi said as she spoke to her cousin on the phone. "Just because I was disciplining my own child. She on some other shit now."

"So what happened again?" Pookie responded, uninterested in talking about Claire but knowing that she had to if she wanted Bobbi to move on to another topic worthy of her attention.

"So I'm changing the baby and she going to come up behind me talking about let her do it," Bobbi continued driving down the road with no destination in mind. "And I wasn't trying to hear shit she was saying because Tristan is my son not hers."

"Hold up Tristan is almost three? He still in pampers?"

"Pookie, please!"

"Finish the story," Pookie responded.

81

"So he hit me in the face with his hand so I hit him back and she lost it," Bobbi lied.

The truth was that Bobbi got jealous about Claire and Tristan's bond. And instead of stepping up to be a good and loving mother, she took to taking her frustrations out on him instead. Claire got so mad that she snatched Tristan out of her hands, and beat Bobbi so badly the cops showed up due to hearing Bobbi's cries. Luckily for Claire she was able to get out of the backdoor before they locked her up.

"But, Bobbi, Tristan is two years old. You can't do no shit like that. He don't know what he's doing to you. He a child."

"I can and I did."

"I think you going overboard, Bobbi, and you know how I feel about Claire so I'm not taking her side. Maybe you should fall back and let her do her thing for Tristan. Don't worry yourself."

"What is that supposed to mean?" she asked jumping in front of someone who was driving too slowly for her. "Why would I do that?"

"We both know that you not the mothering type. I mean think about it for a minute, when was the last time you had the baby without Claire being in the room? She's always taking care of him, and she's doing a good job of it too. Just let her do it and you do you."

"I don't give a fuck if I never touched my baby a day in my life. That's my fucking son, Pook. So if I say I want to change his pamper that's what the fuck it is, and bet not nobody try to stop me either."

"Bobbi, normally I'm with you all the way, but lately I'm thinking that you're doing too much where Tristan is concerned." Pookie sounded frustrated. "I mean, either you want to be a mother or you don't."

"What you mean? You sound stupid over there!"

"I mean you want the tag of mommy but you don't want to put in any work for it. Let that girl do Tristan and you do Red's fine ass. That way everybody will be happy and satisfied."

"Red's fine ass?" Bobbie frowned pulling her car over. "I'm not even talking about him. I'm talking about the baby, and you act like you don't care about my part of the story. This bitch tried to take my son away from me. Do you really think I'm that bad of a mother where I deserve this shit?"

"You don't want to know what I feel about all of this shit."

"Yes I do, Pookie. Fuck is on your mind?"

"First off you know you not into the gay shit, even though you living the lifestyle. I mean she may make you feel good for the moment, but other than that the life is not you. You love men. Yet you over there playing house with a chick you can't even stand. Then you got a nerve to be fucking Red behind her back and then get mad when the girl is taking over your position as mother. You out of line right now, Bobbi. Way out and confused."

83

"You mixing two situations up that ain't even the same. The fact that I'm fucking with a female on the side doesn't mean that she gets to take over my position as mother. And you don't have to like what I do in the bedroom, but if you want me in your life you gotta respect it."

"You need to get your life together, Bobbi. Or you gonna get hurt out here."

"This from a bitch who is fucking with two married men at the same time? You sound like a fool."

"That's cold."

"It ain't about it being cold. It's about it being the truth. Sometimes I think you only like to say certain things to me to bring me down. I mean, if I'm calling you about some real shit then it means that I need your advice, not for you to come down on me."

"You want some advice so here it is. All I can say is that if you want to be a mother, you should act like one first," Pookie said matter of factedly. "You can't make a baby love you who doesn't know you, and I'll leave it at that. Now on to other matters of more importance, what's up with you these days?"

"What the fuck are you talking about? I told you what's up with me."

"I'm off of that. Right now I'm talking about the fact that I almost had to strangle two bitches at Johnny Chicken the other day. I'm in the line waiting on my food and this chick gonna ask me if I was your cousin. So I told the bitch yes."

"Who was she?" Bobbi frowned as she pulled up to the light.

"How the fuck should I know? That's why I'm asking what beef are you into these days. Every time I turn around I got somebody asking me where you are, and if I heard from you."

"I don't know what this bitch is rumbling about," Bobbi admitted turning on the radio. "Nor do I know who she is. What she look like anyway?"

"She was a cute red bone and she was with this pretty dark skin chick. They were starring me down and I started to go in on they asses but I was by myself."

"Did they say what they wanted with me?"

"Only that the were looking for you. You gotta be careful on whatever you're doing out in the streets, Bobbi. Things catching up with you. Their gripe sounded official, and they acted like they was real mad. I got the impression that if you were in the restaurant they may have tried to come at you on some murder shit."

"I wish a bitch would try me in the streets."

"You sure they not one of Red's bitches? They acted jealous."

Just the thought only embarrassed the hell out of Bobbi since she was practically hanging off of his nuts. "Girl, please. Red ain't dumb. He knows what side his bread is buttered on. And I'm not worried about them bitches either. I bought me a gun the other

85

day since I think Vyce is trying to fuck with me. Maybe they with him. Who knows? But I do know this, if either of them bitches step to me it's going to be a mothafucking problem. They not the only ones who can get into some murder shit."

CHAPTER 11

CLAIRE

M eanwhile at R icky's house...

Claire was carrying Tristan on her hip, after begging Bobbi to let her come back home, and help her with him. Ever since Bobbi slapped the baby, and Claire tried to kill her, she hardly fucked with Bobbi. When Bobbi was in the house, to keep the peace, Claire wasn't home. During those times, when Claire was gone, she just prayed to God that Bobbi would be decent and not hurt her own child again.

It was one thing to be a bad mother, but to punish a baby for not liking her was a whole different thing as far as Claire was concerned. Although Claire beat Bobbi's ass for hurting Tristan, it was Bobbi who kept apologizing but Claire wasn't trying to hear it. She wasn't feeling anything about her and suddenly she was no longer attractive in Claire's eyes.

Claire was meeting her mother because Ricky wanted to talk to her about something. When Claire spoke to her on the phone, Ricky sounded as if whatever she wanted to talk to her about was urgent. The moment Claire heard her mother's voice; she wasted no time rushing over to the house with Tristan in tow.

Using her key, Claire opened the back door. "Mommy, I'm here. Sorry I took so long. I had to wait on Bobbi to come home to bring me Tristan's car seat."

When Claire didn't see Ricky in the kitchen, where she spent most of her time braiding hair, she walked toward the living room instead. From where she stood she could hear the TV going. When she bent the corner, her heart felt as if it paused when she saw Humphrey on the sofa beating his long brown dick. Claire had a clear view of his man stick surrounded by extra long gray and black hairs. To make shit worse, the nigga had a nerve to be watching a porno. Claire was so embarrassed her jaw hung and she stiffened.

When she remembered she had the baby with her she covered his eyes, and addressed Humphrey right where he sat. Since she called her mother's name when she came through the backdoor, she was starting to wonder if he didn't do the shit on purpose, even though he was pretending like he didn't see her standing there.

"What the fuck are you doing, nigga? Why the fuck you in my mother's house being perverted?"

Humphrey grabbed the remote control and turned off the TV. He threw it on the couch, hopped up, pulled up his pants and approached her. "Oh shit, I'm

88

so sorry, baby girl." He placed his hands on his hips. "I didn't know you were here. I mean...where..."

"What the fuck were you doing, nigga?" Claire continued. She hated this dude and she wanted a firm answer. She couldn't wait to tell her mother about his bum ass. She knew something was off with him and now she knew what. He was a freak!

"I was just ...cause I..."

"You mean you were beating your old ass dick," she said rolling her eyes. She walked into the kitchen and sat on the barstool at the counter, holding Tristan the entire time. "How trifling can you really be, Humphrey? Why you didn't do that shit in the bedroom? Or in the bathroom?"

Suddenly Humphrey was tired of apologizing for his behavior and it showed all over his face. His eyelids lowered. "For starters you don't live here so I don't have to tell you shit about me or my dick. And secondly, I don't owe you shit. Regardless of how you feel about me, I'm the nigga your mother chose. Now she let you think you can talk to a senior like it's not a—"

"Mothafucka, you ain't no senior," she yelled cutting him off. "You just a mothafucka in here beating his dick while watching my mama's television! What the fuck is wrong with you anyway?"

Humphrey didn't respond. Instead he looked at her, as if he wanted to deal with her in another way. Like wrapping his hands around her neck and squeezing tightly until she stopped breathing. "You know what, back in the day I use to take bitches like you in the alley and leave you dead."

"I'm going to tell—"

He stepped closer to her. "You're going to tell who?" He smirked. "Because I know you weren't getting ready to say your mama. After all, you're grown right? And grown bitches don't go to their mama's and say shit. Now this situation is between you and I, so let it be that way. Besides, your mother is going to be my wife, and that's why she invited you over. Get use to my presence, I'm going to be your pops."

So that was the news. Claire felt sick to her stomach.

"What's going on?" Ricky said stepping into the kitchen. She threw her purse on the counter and pawned the baby's thick curly hair. "Why ya'll looking all crazy?" She looked at Humphrey who backed away from her daughter.

"You want me to tell her or you?" Claire said with an attitude. It was obvious at that moment that she could care less about his threat.

"You know what, I'm sick and tired of your daughter, Ricky," Humphrey said deciding to play the victim. " If we don't make it in this relationship, it will be her fault not mine."

He stormed out of the back door and left them alone in the kitchen. When he was gone Ricky looked at Claire. "What the fuck went down in here? Why he walking out like ya'll just had a fight?"

"Your boyfriend was in here beating his dick! And he did it in front of the baby too, ma! When I said I was going to tell you he low-key threatened my life."

Ricky laughed. "Claire, you need to relax."

"Relax?" Claire responded with widened eyes. She was trembling so much she felt as if she were about to erupt.

"You heard me. Because one of these days you'll stop lying so fucking much, and realize everything ain't about you. I don't know when, but maybe it will be soon."

Claire frowned. "So you think I'm a fucking liar? Really?"

"What am I supposed to think?"— She opened the refrigerator, and grabbed a beer— "You coming at me about my man beating his dick when I know it ain't even the case, besides we just fucked before I went to the bank. I know my nigga, Claire, and you're wrong for trying to break us up."

"I can't believe you can sit over there and actually say that shit to me, ma. I mean are you that pressed for a man that you can't see what's going on before your eyes? Just tell me right now so that I'll know."

"Claire, calm down and stop making everything so extra."

"Making everything extra? Making everything extra," she screamed louder. "I just told you that I saw

91

your boyfriend beating his dick. What is the problem? Huh? Why are you afraid to step to him about it?"

"Claire, just relax"— she gulped half of her beer— "you have been known to see things in a wrong way that's all I'm saying." She slammed the can on the counter.

"You know what, you did the same thing when I was a kid," she said shaking her head. She could feel herself about to cry and she didn't want to give her mother the satisfaction.

"Claire, relax. You just—"

"I just nothing," Claire yelled, causing Tristan to cry. "But I do know one thing I didn't want, and that was daddy fucking me. But let me guess, you don't remember that either huh?"

"Claire, I'm warning you to cut it out." She pointed at her.

"Didn't daddy make me suck his dick? You were always so busy chasing outside dick that you forgot about the one that belonged to you at home. But he didn't, because he forced me to do your job. And you allowed him to do what he wanted to me, because guess what, he paid the bills right? And I begged you"— Tears rolled down her face— "I fucking begged you to help me! I was a kid!"

"Claire, I…"

"You ain't shit, mama. You not shit now and you never will be shit. So fuck you and that creep you fucking, and about to marry. I'm out of your life for good!"

"One day you gonna need me."

"I rather die before I ever come back here. You dead to me."

CHAPTER 12

VYCE

I n an abortion clinic...

Viva lie on the doctor's table with her legs spread eagle. Across the room was Vyce, the love of Viva's life. She would do anything for him, and instead of the man she loved looking inside of her body at the moment, it was Doctor Hamburg. He held firmly onto a tube inserted inside of her vagina that was sucking and pulling at her womb. Tears rolled down her face but they were useless. She was having an abortion.

Viva, who was one of the members of the Lollipop Kidz, had gotten pregnant by Vyce. Because he refused to pull out when he was cumming inside of her, she had become one of the 120 women he fucked raw. And of the 120 women he slept with, she was #47 who found herself in the family way courtesy of him. But Vyce had no intentions on making her a baby mama. He wanted to make her one of his loyal followers instead, and he was doing a good job at it too.

As the cramps ran from the lower part of her stomach, she looked over at Vyce. Her body felt warm all over and her stomach rumbled, giving her the impression that she had to throw up. This was the worst thing that could've ever happened to her. She was in emotional and physical pain.

"Everything is going to be good, my sweet baby," Vyce said to her softly. "Trust me. This is for the better."

The doctor looked behind himself to frown at Vyce. He had zero respect for the nigga, and even less tolerance for him being in his office on a repeated basis to ruin young women's lives and bodies. Still it was because of Vyce that he was able to buy his daughter the E Class Benz she wanted for her eighteenth birthday. He stayed sucking Vyce's embryos into his machine, and the look on Vyce's face told the doctor that he could care less how he felt.

When the procedure was over Viva was escorted to a resting area. In the resting area were a bunch of beds, with thick warm blankets on top of them. Viva was able to lie on a heated mattress, and was fed apple juice and graham crackers to settle her stomach. Because everybody knew Vyce, he was given the VIP treatment and allowed into the room although other men were not. It was so ridiculous that he was even able to lie in a bed beside her, as if he just had his insides suctioned too.

"How do you feel, my sweet baby?" he asked as he ate a cracker next to her. "You look like you don't feel too good."

All Viva could do was cry. She wanted to be strong but she also wanted her baby too. "I feel like shit, Vyce," she sighed. "But I guess I gotta be better huh?"

"I know this ain't something that you wanted to do, and I know you wanted the baby, but I don't want to start our family like this. I imagine our family life would be much sweeter when we are ready, and now is not the time."

"Then how could it be started, Vyce?" she yelled. "I mean I'm so confused right now. One minute you tell me you love me, and the next minute you making me get rid of our child. I don't know what you want from me. You even whispered in my ear and told me you wanted me to have your baby, and to let you cum inside of me. And I did that."

"I know but I realize I'm not ready. Besides, when you have my baby you're going to be my wife," he said whipping out a fake ring that he got from Mexican Larry off of East Capital St. "Can you get with that?"

"Oh my, God, Vyce," she said covering her mouth. "Are you really asking me to...to be your wife?"

He slid the ring on her finger. "I'm dead serious, but we have to talk about something first."

"Anything," she said hoping he wouldn't take back the invitation. Plus she wanted the formal question asked. She wanted to hear the words, will you marry me.

"I'm going to be real with you because I think it's important. I actually wanted you to have my son, my sweet baby," he said looking up into the ceiling for emotional effect. It was a bad acting job at best, but she didn't care. "More than anything I did. But I couldn't trust you based on what I been hearing on the streets lately."

"What you hearing?" she asked anxiously. She turned on her side to look at him. "Because if it's from my cousins Mel and Juniper they just mad because we getting tighter that's all. They don't like that you chose me over them, and they just trying to tear us apart."

"That's not what its about, my sweet baby. You already know you got it over Juniper and Mel."

"Then what is it?"

"I heard that you fucking with the nigga name Bird Reynolds from southwest."

"Bird Reynolds?" she asked confused. "That's impossible! I would never do no shit like that to you. He's not even my speed. He's old in the face, smells like dirt and don't hardly have no money in his pockets. If anything—"

"It doesn't matter, what matters is the fuck that I needed to make sure you weren't having that nigga's baby instead of mine," he said cutting her off. "I mean, if I find out you fucking with him I can't...I can't—"

"Listen to me," Viva said looking into his eyes. "I would never betray you like that, for anybody, Vyce. You were the first person I ever fucked."

"Whatever."

"Vyce, I'm serious, you were my first. I'm not like my cousins and shit. I don't get down like that. I saved myself for you and I love you so much. Can't you tell?"

Vyce did recall her pussy being extra tight, but he was use to it when it came to 18-year olds. Although he would be dishonest if he didn't say that when he fucked a few older joints, that their pussies seemed to grab his dick like a suction cup too, but that was neither here or there.

"If it is true, that you was a virgin, then that means Bobbi and Claire was lying."

"Wait, you talking about Bobbi who got a cousin name Pookie? The Pookie who use to be sucking dick for coinage on the side of the dumpster in back of the 7-11 on South Capitol Street on the southside?"

Vyce laughed to himself. It never ceased to amaze him how young women went so hard at each other. There was no type of loyalty at all, which is why he could get into their minds and pit them against each other. If they stuck together they would be unstoppable but they didn't know it. "Yeah...her."

"She's a fuckin' liar, baby. I would never do you like that. Those bitches just trying to take you away from me, and I'm not going to let 'em."

Vyce stood up and looked down at her. "Well, if that's the case, do something about it then."

"I will," she smirked. "I'll murder both of them bitches with my bare hands. That's on my dead baby!"

CHAPTER 13

BOBBI

In Bobbi and Claire's house...

"Can you tell me what the fuck is wrong with you?" Bobbi asked as she sat at the dining room table with Claire. "You haven't said a word all day to me. I mean I thought we moved past the dumb shit already. Why are we still beefing in our own home?"

"I don't feel like talking right now, Bobbi."

Bobbi looked at the fried chicken on her plate. She picked at the skin, trying to find out if Claire knew something else that she did. If she didn't learn anything else about Claire, she learned that she wasn't as dumb or naive as she thought she was. "Well how was your day today?"

"It was like shit," Claire responded. "Me and my mother still beefing and she trying to get me to come over her house to talk but I don't feel like it. Anyway before I forget, the baby needs new pampers. Did you pick them up like I asked you?"

"Claire, I want to talk about us," Bobbi responded in a frustrated tone. The last thing she was thinking about was her son. Her objective was to get her nails back into Claire's heart so that she could do whatever she wanted with a live-in babysitter, and get into her bank account since Red was draining her dry. "How come whenever we have a conversation it's got to be about Tristan?"

"Because he's relying on us to take care of him that's why. How you sound?"

Bobbi sighed and threw her fork down. "I know he's relying on us, but that ain't what I'm talking about right now. I mean, did somebody say I did something wrong again, because you acting funny? I rather you talk to me instead of sitting over there making assumptions like you do."

Claire looked over at her, trying to figure out where she was going. "I don't know…I mean, are you cheating again?"

"I'm not cheating at all," Bobbi lied. She picked up her fork and picked through her food. "I never cheated a day in my life and I never will. But can you talk to me please? And tell me what's going on?"

"It really is about my mother, Bobbi," Claire said. "I saw some shit the last time I was at her house that fucked me up. And I don't think I can get past it this time."

"What was it?"

"So I go over my mother's house with Tristan because she said she wanted to talk to me, but when I get there she wasn't home. I walked into the living room and see her boyfriend beating his dick on the so-

101

fa. Bobbi, I was so fuckin' mad. And when I brought it up to my mother, she had the nerve to tell me that—"

"We should go to the movies or something tomorrow," Bobbi interrupted. "We haven't done nothing together in a long time. If you want I can get Pookie to watch Tristan and everything so the night can be special."

Claire frowned. "Go to the movies? Did you hear what I just said to you? I was bearing my heart."

Bobbi didn't hear shit she was spitting, because she zoned out a long time ago and wasn't listening. She didn't give a fuck about Claire. As usual her two-second mind went off to thoughts about her. Bobbi was so selfish that somebody could be crying over the death of their mother, and she would find a way to bring the topic back to herself.

"I heard what you said," she lied. "You said…uh…you were talking about…I mean…"

"This is why I don't fuck with you," Claire said wiping the corners of her mouth with the napkin. "You too fucking egotistical, Bobbi. I fucking hate that shit about you."

"Claire, you need to fucking relax. Here I was, trying to make us a nice dinner and this is what happens. I can't fucking stand you. Just because I couldn't hear what you were saying don't mean I wasn't listening. I didn't want to be rude and ask you to speak up so I waited until you finished talking."

When Claire's cell phone rang she answered. "Where you at, Natalie?"

"I'm out in front of the house."

"Well I'm coming to open the door now." Claire stood up from the table and walked toward the front door.

"Who the fuck is that?" Bobbi asked following her. "Because I told you I didn't want that bitch around my house after she cussed me out on the phone."

"Sorry, but it is Natalie."

Claire opened the door and let Natalie inside of the house, and the moment she did Bobbi like to have lost her mind. "I was talking to you, Claire," Bobbi roared. "And you acting like I'm a fucking joke. What is going on with you these days?"

When the baby started crying in the living room due to Bobbi screaming Claire walked toward him. Natalie was right on her tail along with Bobbi. Claire lifted the baby out of the playpen to calm him down.

"Claire, we were having a conversation that I would like to finish."

"Bobbi, I need you to relax, you know he's scared of you after that last situation when you hurt him."

"Bitch, do you think I'm some fucking joke?" Bobbi frowned. "I'm fucking talking to you and I want us to continue our conversation in private. And instead

103

of respecting me, you in here holding court with this chick."

"Like Claire said, you need to calm down," Natalie added sitting on the sofa.

Bobbi walked up to her slowly. She balled her fists up and looked down at her. "What did you just say to me? In my house?"

"I said that you need to calm the fuck down. It ain't like you didn't hit the baby already for something he didn't do. I know you not about to do it again, not with me standing here anyway."

"So you told this chick my business?" Bobbi asked Claire. She was beyond furious.

Claire ignored her.

In anger Bobbi considered how she could best hurt her. Not only was she pissed that Natalie felt she was within her constitutional rights to speak on her business, in her house at that, but she also didn't like her. She never had and never would. Bobbi could tell by looking into Natalie's eyes that she was digging on Claire, even if Claire didn't know. The messed up part was that since she was fucking Red, she shouldn't care, but why did it hurt so much?

"Natalie, I'm telling you as nicely as possible, you better get up and get out of my house in the next five seconds, not a second more."

"And if I don't," Natalie said standing up.

"Then I'm going to stomp you into the fibers of my carpet. You don't know me bitch, but the middle name is Bonds, as in Barry Bonds, and I'm vicious with a baseball bat."

"You know what, I don't have time for this irregular ass shit." Natalie walked around Bobbi and kissed the baby on the forehead. "Claire, I'll talk to you later."

"Don't put your fucking lips on my baby," she said snatching Tristan from Claire's arms. Immediately he cried out in pain due to the force she exhibited with him once again.

At this point Claire had enough with her being violent with Tristan. That was the final straw.

CHAPTER 14

CLAIRE

In Bobbi and Claire's living room...

"Here, put this on your hand, Claire," Natalie said handing her a pack of peas. Natalie sat next to her on the couch. "I can't believe you dropped that girl like that. I know them your peoples, but I'm five seconds from calling child protective services on that bitch, Claire. That's on Jesus Christ our savior!

"I could've killed her, Natalie," Claire said placing the peas on her swollen hand. "I could've literally smashed her face into the back of her skull. I tried but Tristan kept crying because he was scared."

"You could have?" she joked. "You did smash her face in."

"I'm serious," Claire yelled. "I wanted to murder her. I fucking can't believe she snatched Tristan by his arm like that. I mean who the fuck do she think she is? She don't love that baby like I do. She never did and she never will."

Natalie placed her hand on Claire's knee. "Claire, maybe you should come to the realization that he is not your son. I mean, I know you love him, believe me I do, but he's not yours. He never was and he never will be. So let it go. I mean if anything you can have your own baby. Shit, you still young."

Claire's shoulders hunched over. "I can't have no baby," Claire responded walking away from her. "You don't understand."

"What you mean you can't? Shit, I know at least two fine ass niggas right now on speed dial who would kill to fuck you and have a—"

"You don't understand," she said throwing the peas down on the floor. "I can't have any babies, Natalie. I mean I can't hold them in my body. I wish I could but I can't. So Tristan was like my baby, and now he's gone. After what I did to Bobbi she never gonna let me see that baby again. If you didn't see her snatch the baby arm, and threaten to call the police to report her, she would've called the cops again on me to put me out."

Natalie walked up to her. "The way I see it you still don't have a problem, because if it's a baby you want," she said rubbing her hair backwards, "then I can do that for you. Just say the word, Claire."

"Natalie, what are you talking about?" Claire walked away, and Natalie followed her again.

"I don't want you to have to depend on that bitch for nothing, Claire. So if you want a baby, that ain't nothing. I know what I'm saying but I want you to hear me too, and believe me."

Claire looked into her eyes. "And why would you do something like that? You don't even know me that well."

Natalie stepped so close to Claire she couldn't move anymore. "Because I love you." She kissed her on the lips. "Don't you see that? Can't you tell? Because I know Bobbi can. That's why she hates me so much."

Claire couldn't lie. She felt a tingling sensation coursing through her body. Claire felt alive again even though she never looked at her friend like that.

Natalie sensing Claire's attraction toward her went in for a tongue kiss. As their lips pressed together Claire led her to the couch and pushed her down. Natalie unable to wait tore Claire's clothes off. And before Claire could take control of the situation, or back off, she already had her pants down at her ankles.

"Damn, you going hard," Claire whispered. "I don't know about this shit. I mean you're my friend."

"You have no idea how badly I've been wanting you, Claire." She kissed her inner thigh. "Please don't fight me or deny. Let me make you feel good. You deserve me."

Claire bit down on her bottom lip as she gave into the feeling. "But why you like me like this? You never said anything to me before, Natalie. This shit is crazy."

"Because I knew you'd say no, and that you were in love with Bobbi. So I waited for her to fuck up and she did."

Before Claire could refuse, Natalie was kissing her pussy. Claire ran her hands through Natalie's hair and widened her legs. Claire was just about to cum when Bobbi came through the door without the baby in her arms.

"What the fuck is going on?" Bobbi looked at Claire and then Natalie who was on her knees between Claire's legs. "What are ya'll doing in my fucking house?"

Claire jumped up and said, "Uh...we were...I mean...where is Tristan?"

"Bitch, what the fuck is going on in my house?" Bobbi repeated.

Natalie wiped her mouth and said, "You a smart girl, I mean what do it look like?" she smirked.

Before Claire could silence Natalie, Bobbi came down on Natalie's head with the baseball bat that she kept next to the door.

CHAPTER 15

VYCE

At Vyce's house...

An open window brought with it a cool breeze that entered Vyce's dining room. He was sitting across the table eyeing Tya with discontent in his eyes. His patience had run thin with her because she was the third part of his plan, and she wasn't working out. She had better say something that he wanted to hear or there would be hell to pay.

"I found out some information," she said swallowing a piece of overcooked steak. When it came to cooking Tya was the world's worst and she knew it. "I wish I could find more for you, Vyce, but it's the only thing I could come up with."

He exhaled in frustration. Tya was nothing without her excuses. "What is it?" he asked, tearing into the tough meat.

"They are throwing a birthday party for Tristan, Bobbi's son. And lately Bobbi and Claire are spending less time in DC and more time in Delaware, so if you don't meet them there, you probably won't be able to find them anywhere else. That's why it's hard for me to get their location out there."

For a moment he considered the fact that Tristan was supposed to be his child. But he washed the thought from his mind when he recalled how many people gave him the "T" on the baby, by saying that Tristan looked more like the talk show host Oprah Winfrey than he did him.

He threw the fork on the table. "Where is this party?"

"They having it here in, DC, at a museum. It's supposed to be really nice too, and a lot of people are going to be there." She wiped her hands on the napkin in her lap and looked over at him. "It's the only thing I could find out for you right now, Vyce. I really am sorry."

"I guess the party would be elaborate, considering they got me for all of my money," he scowled. "I swear I can't believe I let them bitches catch me slipping, and no matter what I do, I can't put the shit out of my mind. I was stupid! What the fuck is wrong with me? I mean, why didn't I see them for who they really were? Gold diggers."

"You didn't do anything wrong, Vyce" -- she wiped her mouth with the napkin and rushed over to him on the other side of the table -- "You trusted them and they burnt you. If anything you're the victim in this shit, because they took advantage of your generos-

111

ity. You're far from stupid, if you ask me you're the smartest man I know."

Tya laid it on thick because she knew the bottom of his boot had her name written all over it. Not only did she side with Claire and Bobbi, two women who she met through Vyce, she stabbed him in the back and she knew at some point she had to pay.

"If that's the case, why did you betray me?"

She knelt at his feet. "Because I was mad, Vyce. I felt betrayed."

"For what?" he frowned. "The only thing I ever did was take care of you. Bitch, you didn't have to ask for shit when you were in my company. If you wanted money, I gave it to you. When you wanted new clothes, I bought them for you. Half of the designer purses in your closet are courtesy of my generosity. And you were mad? What the fuck do you have to be mad about?"

"I was mad because I wanted you to myself, and I realized I couldn't have you. You don't know how it made me feel to come over your house that night, only to see Claire opening the door. And then later to find out that Bobbi was living there with you too! When you knew me way before them bitches? Why didn't you move me in, instead of them? I was fucked up, baby, and I made a bad move and got up with two chicks I should not have trusted. And not a day goes by when I don't think about my mistake."

He rubbed her dreads backwards and looked down at her face. "You know what, I always thought you were beautiful."

Her body trembled. Tya knew that where there was a compliment from Vyce, there was often a blow to the face too. So she braced herself. "T-thank you baby," she stuttered. "I appreciate--"

And just as she thought he came down on her face with a closed fist. Tya tried to crawl away but he gripped a fistful of her luscious dreadlocks and dragged her toward the basement. Once he was inside he locked the door, and pushed her down the basement steps.

Her legs broke immediately but he didn't care. Vyce hated himself for being played by women and he was not going to allow it to happen again.

Vyce beat Tya so badly that she was bruised, swollen and confused about what happened. When he was done he looked down at her and said, "Now what do you have to say?

She rolled over and looked up at him. She was weak, bloodied, in pain and out of energy. "Thank you."

"Thank you for what?"

"For putting me in my place, daddy. I...I love you."

"I know you do, my sweet baby. I know."

****

Vyce sat across from Viva of the Lollipop Kidz, at Friday's restaurant. She had a big box on the table and he wondered what it was. But because it was more important for him to act as if he didn't give a fuck, as opposed to anything else, he kept his curiosity in check.

"How was your day?" She said trying to strike up conversation. "Everything okay?"

"It was fine," he said dryly, sipping his Hennessy. "Pretty uneventful."

"I was thinking about you," she smiled. "I had a dream that me and you are going to be so good together, Vyce. Like everything is going to work out between us.

"Good for you," he shrugged.

She swallowed. "Vyce, are you gonna stay mad at me forever?" she frowned. "I mean, you gonna feel like shit when you see that my love for you is true. I'm being so honest, I really was a virgin and whoever told you that I wasn't is lying. They are just trying to keep us a part." Vyce seemed uninterested. "Look at what I got you." She pushed the box in his direction.

"You can't get me nothing I can't get for myself, shawty," he laughed. "So stay in your fucking lane." He thought it was amusing how she tried to use his game on him, by buying him a gift.

Her feelings were extremely hurt. "Can you at least look at it?"

Vyce smirked, and grabbed the box. When he opened it he almost choked when he saw a pair of Foamposites that he had been trying to get his hands on forever in his size. Not only were the shoes expensive, getting them was virtually impossible so Viva had to have gone through a lot of work.

He slammed the box closed and slid them back over to her. "These are nice but they ain't what I want."

The smile was removed from her face, and her shoulders dropped, followed by her head. "Then what can I do to make you know that I love you, Vyce? I'm seriously willing to do anything you want. Just say the word."

"You wouldn't be willing to do what I want, because you're too young to understand my world."

"Vyce, on everything I love, I will do anything you want me to do. Just tell me. Please."

His dick hardened again with the news. "Okay, well I been thinking about what happened with the baby. And I realized that I really wanted that child because I can't stop thinking about it; you know what I'm saying? And to think, that I couldn't have our baby because some bitches lied burns me up. You feel me?"

Her eyes widened and a huge smile spread over her face. "I swear to God I do! And it makes me feel so good that you are thinking about our baby too. Because its the only thing on my mind now."

"Then what do you think I want done about it, Viva?"

She shrugged. "You want to have another baby? Because I would be willing to do that if that's what you want."

"I'm not trying to have no nother baby right now," he frowned. She sounded stupid. "Not until we correct our first problem."

She pouted. "Then what is it, daddy?"

"I want you to take care of them bitches that lied. I want them dealt with, Viva. Are you big enough to handle that?"

"What…I mean, how?"

"So all of the things you were telling me, at the clinic was just a way to get me to think you were hard? Is that what you're saying? Now I'm not dealing with no weak ass bitches no more. I'm only dealing with women who prove to go the distance for me. Can you do that?"

Viva knew from the look in his eyes that he meant business, She also knew that if she wanted him, she had to go all the way. "Vyce, I will do anything you want me to do, including murder."

CHAPTER 16

BOBBI

I n W ashington D C at R ed's house...

Bobbi grabbed Tristan out of the car seat. The moment she took the baby into her arms, he started whimpering as usual when she held him. Instead of having compassion for the baby, and realizing he was wearing a wet diaper for the past six hours, Bobbi took to yelling into the baby's eyes.

"You the whiniest baby I ever met in my life, dang!" she yelled walking up the steps leading toward Red's door. "The least you could do is act like a boy instead of a dumb bitch! If I wanted a girl I would've had one, instead of some faggy ass baby like you."

Tristan didn't understand what his mother was talking about, but he didn't like how she yelled at him either. So he showed her how he felt about her by kicking his arms and screaming louder in her face. He would stiffen his body on and off so much that it was hard to carry him.

"Bobbi, what you doing with that baby?" Ovaline, Red's next-door neighbor asked. She walked

117

up to them and placed her hand on the baby's face. He silenced instantly. "Isn't he precious?"

"Girl, fuck being precious. I swear I don't know how much more of this I can take. I'm about to lose my mind, Ovaline."

"Give me that baby, chile, before you make him lose his mind first."

Bobbi threw the baby into her arms so fast that his forehead knocked against her chin. And if anybody knew anything about baby's heads they would know that Ms. Ovaline was in serious pain.

"Who's baby is this?" she asked ignoring the soreness by looking into the baby's beautiful eyes. She rubbed her chin.

"What you mean who baby is this," Bobbi replied smacking her lips. "You knew I had a baby right?"

"Chile, I ain't never seen you with no baby since I've been knowing you. So no, I didn't realize you were a mother. Now where is his pampers? The child is about five pounds heavier than what he should be because of his diaper alone."

Bobbi reached in the bag and handed the woman the diaper. She was sick and tired of people telling her how to be a good mother, especially when they were right. Shit, if you asked Bobbi's opinion she was the best mother in the world. She never hit him accept those two times he was with Claire, and she made sure he ate at least once a day. She wanted the "Mother of the Century" award instead of the ridicule and advice that people continued to give her.

"Well, I'm going to take him to my place for a little while. You go on over there and see your man. Don't worry, your son is safe with me."

Bobbi sprinted into Red's house before the old broad could change her mind, and decided not to watch the baby. When she opened Red's door he was in the middle of the living room sitting on the sofa holding a major attitude.

"What's wrong with you?" She asked throwing the baby bag on the sofa, as the door slammed behind her. Bobbi forgot to give it to Ovaline and made mental notes to take it to her later.

"You know what's wrong with me, Bobbi," he said looking seriously into her eyes. "So don't fuck with me right now, because I'm not in the mood."

Bobbi wrecked her mind trying to think about what could possibly be his problem. "I'm not going to lie, Red, you do better just telling me what your beef is," she admitted. "Cause right now I'm stuck and have no idea what I could've done to you. If anything you still owe me for even coming over here, considering how you let them niggas rob me."

"You still talking about that dumb shit?" he said. "Bitch, once you took this dick again you gave up the right to bring up that old ass story. What I want to know is why you got that loud ass baby outside of my house making all that noise? Huh? That shit's embarrassing."

She frowned. *I know damn well that this nigga not talking about his own child like that.* She knew she treated Red like he was king, and because of it he felt like he could talk to her any kind of way, but this took the cake. "By the loud ass baby do you mean Tristan? Your son?"

He waved her off. "Whatever his name is."

"Red, you know I'm the sole provider of Tristan now." She sat next to him on the sofa. "I mean, me and Claire not together no more because of the last fight we had when I busted one of her friends in the head. Anyway ain't that what you told me you wanted? Me and the baby alone?"

"Bobbi, I'm not going to lie, you with this baby all of the time is not working for me no more. And it never will work for me. I like a woman who can come and go as she pleases. The way you rolling with this baby got me thinking that we an *old* couple before we have a chance at having *young* fun."

"So what you saying?"

He exhaled. "I been thinking a lot about this, so hear me out. I mean, maybe you should give the baby up for adoption."

It was a good thing that the couch was up under her because she sure enough would've hit the floor. "Adoption?" she placed her hand over her heart. "Red, do you know what you saying?" She got up and walked away from him.

"Yes, baby," he walked over to her. "Think about it for a minute, if you give the baby up for adoption, then me and you can *do us* like we always talked about. We can get our barbershop up and running and..."

"But he's your son, Red," she said in a low voice. "Ain't that good for nothing?"

"To you it may be good for something, but I don't want no kid, Bobbi. I want you, and the life I know we could have."

Bobbi felt like dried shit was stuck to her face. She couldn't believe that he was putting her in this type of predicament, and more importantly that he didn't care. Yes, Tristan got on her ever lasting nerves. And yes she didn't like his whiney ass too much, but at the end of the day she still pushed him out of her pussy. If nothing else, didn't that make him their responsibility?

Instead of telling the nigga to eat a dick she said, "I gotta think about what you asking me, Red. I mean, it seems so cold to do the little guy like that. If I knew you were going to carry the situation in this way, I would've let Claire take him. You were the one who convinced me that I needed to take control of my kid, and that's what I did."

He rolled his eyes. "Maybe I made a mistake. And maybe you still can let her have him." He grabbed her hand. "People make bad decisions all the time, and maybe we did too by throwing her out of our lives."

Our lives? This dude must be on crack!

"Where is this coming from, Red?" she asked suspiciously. "I know you, and if I know nothing else its that you always have an angle."

"I'm wearing my heart on my shoulder, Bobbi. What you see is what I'm giving. Ain't no other angles over here."

She walked away and placed her hands over her face. "But she may not want him now." She dropped her hands. "Claire ain't talked to me since she left the house."

"And yet you thought she was a queen." He shook his head. "You see what happens when you need her the most? She abandons you." He shook his head again. "Well let me go make us some drinks, and when I come back we'll go over the pros and cons of adoption. It looks like it's our only option."

When he was gone she thought about what really happened the last time she saw Claire. Because Bobbi got ridiculous, and hit Natalie over the head with the bat, resulting in her having to go to the hospital, Claire left her for good. Not only did Bobbi miss Claire a little, but she also missed how she cared for Tristan when Bobbi didn't feel like it, which was all of the time.

Thanks to Red, Bobbi was so confused now.

The moment her thoughts floated on her old relationship, her phone rang. She almost turned a different race when she saw Claire's name pop up on the screen. It was as if she heard her thoughts. "Hello," Bobbi said excitedly.

"Hey, Bobbi," Claire said dryly.

Always on some slick shit, Bobbi got up and walked out of the house. She didn't want Red coming back into the living room and overhearing the conversation. "Hey, Claire. What you up to?"

"Making it," she responded. "How's the baby?"

Bobbi was so angry she was asking about Tristan she hung up the phone, although she regretted it moments later. When Claire called back Bobbi knew she had to get her life together along with a good lie on why she hung up before she messed up everything again.

"What happened?" Claire asked.

"The call dropped," Bobbi lied. "I'm sorry."

"Cool, but look, I wanted to tell you that even though we broke up, I'm still here for Tristan. You don't have to do it on your own, Bobbi. I said I would be in your corner to help with him, and I mean it. You still got me."

Bobbi didn't know whether to be grateful or irritated. Claire seemed more interested in the baby than anything else, and she knew she shouldn't be surprised because Claire was a Tristan cheerleader from the start. "Thank you," Bobbi responded.

123

"And I'm going to be there at his birthday party too. Don't worry about nothing, Bobbi, I'm here. I got a feeling this party is going to be his most memorable."

Bobbi was silent for a moment. "You still love me?" she asked Claire.

Claire didn't respond.

"Claire, do you still love me?"

Claire cleared her throat and said, "Not for nothing, Bobbi, but I'm not feeling you in that way no more. And you gotta respect that. Okay?"

CHAPTER 17

CLAIRE

O ver N atalie's house in D elaware...

Claire propped a pillow behind Natalie's neck, as Natalie struggled to get comfortable in bed. Ever since Bobbi took to beating her in the back of the head, which resulted in five stitches and a patch missing from her hair weave, Claire became her slave. In Claire's opinion the best thing about the situation was that Natalie suffered memory loss, and had no idea why she was fucked up and in the bed.

"You comfortable?" Claire asked as she sat on the edge of the bed.

"Kinda," Natalie moaned a little. "I'm just happy you're here to help me, girl. Because I don't know what I would do without your help. You know?"

"You know I wouldn't be any place else but here," Claire admitted. "So don't even worry about that."

Especially since it was my dumb ass girlfriend who hit you.

"I just wish I could remember what happened to me," Natalie said to her. "I mean, one minute we fool-

125

ing around, and the next minute I'm in the hospital. I know you know what happened so why are you holding back? Did Bobbi do this shit to me?"

Claire felt guilty for lying to Natalie but she felt she had too. She wasn't certain but something told Claire that if Natalie knew that Bobbi got one in on her, there would be a war of the bitches in the neighborhood. In her opinion she was preventing the drama by not telling the entire story.

"It's like I told you, Natalie, we were playing around and you fell backwards on the table and hit your head. That's what happened, and Bobbi didn't have shit to do with it. She wasn't even at the house when that happened."

Natalie eyed her suspiciously. "Damn, well, at least we were having fun when it happened I guess."

Claire smiled halfway. "Yeah, we were."

"So what you gonna do today, Claire? I'm feeling better so I figured that I can make us a couple of chicken pot pies with rice and—"

"I gotta go pick up Tristan from Bobbi's."

The smile was wiped clean off of Natalie's face. "Fuck you mean you gotta go pick up Tristan? I thought you said it was over between ya'll. Why would you keep putting up with that girl when you don't have to? It's like you're a glutton for punishment or something."

Claire extended her hand and said, "Hold up, where all the animosity coming from all of a sudden?"

"It ain't about animosity! It's about the fact that you still messing with a bitch when we supposed to be together now."

Claire's heart thumped and her jaw hung. "Natalie, I never said me and you were together. I mean we did the grown people thing but that was about it. You know that. I can't jump into another situation just yet. I have to see about my house, and my family. When I do that, then maybe we can talk about what's going on with us."

Natalie jumped her half cracked head out of the bed and stomped around the bedroom. "You are so fucking stupid! So fucking dumb!" she placed her hands on her hips. "How could you play yourself like that? What about that girl makes you want to still be her flunky? Please help me understand."

"Natalie, maybe you should lay back down," Claire said with an attitude. "Because you five seconds from blowing a gasket."

"Don't tell me to lay back down! I want you to answer the question and I want you to answer it now. How can you take care of her baby when you know how she treats you? Huh?"

"How Bobbi treats me doesn't have anything to do with you, Natalie."

"Yes it does, because when she hurts your feelings it's going to be me that you come running back too."

127

"I can't believe it, you're acting just like her right now"— Claire got up and walked across the room to put her watch on— "I'm going to leave. I gotta make it back to the house to meet Bobbi anyway. You need to relax and get some more rest."

"Claire, I'm sorry I'm yelling at you," Natalie said snatching the watch out of Claire's hand. "But Bobbi is playing the Olympics with your mind right now. And as long as you let her, she'll continue to try to get over on you. Don't you see that shit?"

"Again, that's my business not yours. The sooner you realize that the better off you'll be."

"You don't see it do you? You really don't see the bigger picture."

"What I see is that you need to give me my space," she grabbed her watch, and placed it on her arm.

"So just because I care about you I'm crazy?"

"No, you wrong for acting crazy when you know how I feel about my son. That's what you're wrong about."

In a low voice she said, "Claire, that baby is not yours. Do you understand that?"

"He is mine," Claire yelled pointing in her face. "And that's why me and you will never do anything but fuck. Because you don't understand that when it comes to Tristan, there's nothing nobody can tell me. He's the only person in this world that smiles whenever I walk in the room, no matter how bad he feels."

"I smile when you walk in the room."

"Natalie, you got so many cracks in your forehead right now from frowning that your face looks like a DC street. Trust me, you don't smile every time I come into the room."

Natalie sighed. "So give me time to be good with this relationship you gotta have with her son then. But don't carry me like I don't matter at all."

"There's nothing I can do to change how you feel. You'll never know how much he means to me, and I'm good with that, but you're going to have to be good with losing me too."

When Claire's phone rang she grabbed it out of her purse, which was sitting on the bed. It was Bobbi. "Bobbi, I'm on my way right now."

"It's not that."

"What's wrong?"

"Tristan's sick, Claire. You gotta come now, please, because I don't know what to do."

CHAPTER 18

VYCE

A t E rica's house...

Vyce was laying butt ass naked in the dark on top of Erica's 800-thread count sheet set. He was smoking a blunt, and enjoying the view. He was watching Erica, Whiz's other baby mother, dance in front of him at the foot of the bed. He had been wanting to fuck her from the moment Whiz showed him her face, and it didn't hurt that her body was sick. The only foul part in Vyce's opinion was that he had to wait until his man died to step to her.

"Why you looking at me like that boy?" Erica asked moving her hips from left to right. "You act like you want to lick me clean."

"I'm looking like that because you a bad bitch," he said releasing a cloud of white smoke from his lungs, and into the air. "You got my dick hard as shit right now."

She frowned and stopped moving. "Why you gotta keep talking to me like that?"

"Talking to you like what?"

"Like I'm some second hand bitch?" She flopped down onto the edge of the bed. "I'm a grown as woman, Vyce. Not some young ass girl you usually fuck with. You gotta come way better than that if you want to keep my pussy wet."

He sighed. Early on Vyce assumed that he only enjoyed young bitches, because of their young minds and naive ways. But it was becoming evident that what he really liked was pussy. Good pussy. If a dog, cat, mouse or wall had a pussy, Vyce would no doubt fuck it. His only downfall was that older women didn't fall prey as easy to his games as their younger counterparts. Although it made winning the older ones over more challenging and sweeter, at the end of the day it was a lot of hard work when all he really wanted to do was bust a nut.

"I know you not young, Erica, and I wasn't trying to come at you like that. I'm a hood nigga, and hood niggas speak their mind. I thought that was one of the things you were attracted to. "

"I'm not young," she repeated with raised eyebrows. After everything he said, that one piece wrecked her mind. "I might not be real young but I'm not no old ass crow either."

"Never said that," he gripped the back of her head and pulled her face toward his. "Now stop being a downer. All I want to do is have a little fun with you and pass some time."

131

"Before we get into all of that I want to know where you've been lately, Vyce? It seems like every time I call you, you don't answer the phone. And instead of returning my call, you'll wait days later to hit me up and ask what I'm doing. I mean are we an item or what?"

Vyce rolled his eyes and sighed. "Why you doing this shit now? Damn! All a nigga want to do is see you, Erica"— he scratched his balls— "and spend a little time. And you in here acting like a female."

"Vyce, I am a female."

"You know what the fuck I mean."

"What I know is that you aren't trying to answer the question. Are you with me or not?"

"You know I am, Erica. I'm here right?"

"Then, show and prove, nigga. Start by coming by and seeing me more."

"You sound crazy," he laughed, "I take care of my man's daughter as if she were my own. And whenever you need something I'm only a phone call away. So don't even try to front on me."

"I'm not talking about the dress socks you brought over here for us the other day, Vyce, I'm talking about you doing right by me. I don't know if you realize it or not, but I still turn heads. Niggas be checking for me hard all the time."

"I know that, why you think I'm over here?" he scratched his balls again, and then grabbed her hand.

"Now stop fucking around, and get over here and on top of me."

He pulled her into his body and she fell on top of him. The moment she looked into his eyes her pussy got juicy. But Vyce was not a fool. He noticed the lustful look in her eyes, and he wanted to get his rocks off before he fucked her and she got hers first. So he whipped his dick out of his pants and smiled.

"You always want me to suck that big old dick of yours don't you?" Erica announced.

"You know what it is, mama." He waved it back and forth. "And I haven't met a female who has done it better than you."

Never shy when it came to stick licking, Erica lowered her head and ran her tongue alongside his dick's shaft. His back trembled and he couldn't wait to bust off into her mouth. A second between her lips and he knew he wouldn't be able to control himself, so it was best to get her to do something else that he loved so that he could prolong the feeling.

"Erica, how 'bout you do that other thing I like."

Instead of frowning like most women would, Erica winked at him. That was one thing that could be said about her, as opposed to Diane, Whiz's other baby mother. Erica loved the kinky shit. It did her heart good to please him in ways that she imagined other women wouldn't. She considered the dirty act would increase her market value, and in Vyce's opinion she was right. If he had a few moments to spare, he would

133

almost always spend them with her as opposed to Diane.

Erica crawled down to Vyce's lower body. Then she grabbed his foot. She started licking his toes until his dick was so stiff, large veins ran along the shaft and it dripped with pre-cum. She ran her tongue between each big toe and sucked long and hard on the big one. Although it was not in the cards to beat his dick before she got started, she was just too good at the toe sucking for him not to take advantage.

"Damn, you the baddest."

Erica didn't respond. She didn't need the compliments or encouragement. She really enjoyed the freaky shit and she did better when he left her alone and to her job.

"I'm not going to be able to take it much longer, Erica. You gotta get up here and give me some of that quiet."

Erica crawled on top of him, and instead of riding his dick like he suggested, she swallowed his stick whole. Vyce gripped at the covers in an effort to control his orgasm but it was difficult. It wasn't even a minute later before he exploded into her throat. Erica loved every minute of it.

When she saw he was still stiff she was about to ride him until her phone rang. "Don't answer that shit right now, Erica," he said pulling her hand. "You tending to me right now, and I'm not done with you yet."

"Just one minute," she said hopping off of the bed. "When that phone rings it means it's an emergency. I'll be right back with you for part two. Don't worry."

"Well hurry the fuck back, you blowing me." He was always annoyed when he didn't get what he wanted. "I'm trying to get into that hole next."

She rolled her eyes and playfully answered the phone. "Hello."

"Hey, Erica, it's me, Diane."

Erica sighed because although they had gotten cordial since Whiz was murdered, she still didn't deal with her too much. After all, they both fucked and loved the same man, even though he was dead. Whiz meant everything to both of them and they vowed to keep their kids together, so that they would know one another.

"What's up, girl? I'm kind of busy right now but I got a few seconds." She looked over at Vyce and blew a kiss.

"Oh really? What you doing?"

"Ain't nothing really, just sitting over here fucking around with Vyce's fine ass."

The moment Vyce heard his name his eyes expanded as wide as the planet Earth. Why was she mentioning his name? The agreement was that they would keep their arrangement secret from all others, because nobody would understand how they felt for one another. And now she was mouth flexing to some broad on

135

the phone he didn't know. His only hope was that it wasn't Diane, the other bitch he was sleeping with on the side.

The crazy part was that Vyce had no business being over there anyway. He was supposed to be working up the Lollipop Kidz, so that they could rid his life of Claire and Bobbi once and for all. But the freak in him took too many liberties, and he felt invincible. That's why they were able to take him for his paper before, because he often let his guard down.

"Vyce?" Diane said with an attitude on the phone. "What my nigga doing over your house?"

"Your nigga?" Erica frowned, still tasting his toes and cum in her mouth. "Me and him been together for months now. When you get with him?"

"Erica, now you know I don't fuck with you like that, but I wouldn't even play like this. On my mother that dude and me been cruising ever since we buried our baby father, God rest his soul. I'm not sure, but I think Vyce really trying to play us."

Erica frowned. "Well I got games for niggas like that. I'll get at you later." She hung up the phone and Vyce already knew what went down. His cover had been blown, and now he had to deal with the drama.

"Well let me get up out of here," he said placing his boxers on, followed by his jeans. "I gotta see these dudes about my money out in the streets. I didn't know it was so late."

He was gum flapping the entire time but Erica wasn't paying him any mind. She was to busy loading her pistol and there was about to be hell to pay.

The moment she had it in her hand, she aimed and pointed it at him. She wasn't one for talking, or holding a gun and not using it. The first bullet crashed the Jesus picture on the wall. But the next was going to pierce his flesh if she had anything to do with it.

CHAPTER 19

BOBBI

At the dining room table at Bobbi and Claire's house...

Bobbi was sitting on the opposite side of the dining room table from Claire. Tristan was in Claire's arms and she couldn't keep her eyes off of him. Even though it hadn't been too long since she last saw him, it felt like ages. She worried nonstop about him when she couldn't lay eyes on him. She wondered if he was well, or if Bobbi was feeding him the right food that wouldn't cause his stomach to be upset. In her heart she was his mother, not Bobbi.

Although the only person Claire was thinking about was Tristan, Bobbi was on a mission. To get back into Claire's good graces, Bobbi prepared a four star meal of steak, garlic mashed potatoes and asparagus. She was pulling out all of the stops to get what she wanted, Claire back under her control.

"He doesn't look that sick to me, Bobbi," Claire said looking up at her, as she played with Tristan's fingers. "You sure he was sick instead of just having gas? Because they can still be upset when they're gassy too."

"He was coughing earlier," Bobbi responded swallowing a fork full of mashed potatoes. "I do know what sick looks like you know?"

"I'm not saying that. I just want to know what's wrong with him. I mean, why isn't he coughing now?"

"Please don't tell me you would think that I would lie on my son like that?" Bobbi threw her fork down and it banged against her plate. "If I said he was sick he was sick, Claire. I mean, why would I lie to you? It ain't like you weren't coming over here anyway."

"Yeah, but I was coming to get him and leave. You told me he was sick so that meant I couldn't take him out of the house, and I had to stay. I'm not pointing fingers, but if you ask me it does look suspect."

Bobbi rolled her eyes and folded her hands over her chest. "Claire, why are we doing this to each other? I mean, we use to be so close. So tight." She leaned into the table. "It seems like you changed all of a sudden. You not the same."

"I'm the same person. The only thing I'm not doing anymore is taking anybody else's shit, and that goes for you too. At the end of the day you made a mistake when you played me for soft by telling me you wanted to fuck dudes, and I had to call you on it."

"Claire, please."

139

"You assumed that because I loved you, that I would let you walk all over me like I allowed Vyce to. But you were wrong weren't you? You found out that I'm stronger now than I was when we first met. Vyce changed all that shit about me. From here on out I'm making decisions not to press anybody who don't want me."

"You weren't the only one in that relationship with him," Bobbi responded with an attitude. "Vyce changed me too you know, but it doesn't mean I'm going to treat you any different."

"I can't speak on you, or what he did for your life. I just know that for me, he made me stronger. I'm not young and dumb anymore, Bobbi. I'm too smart for all that shit. Which is why when I look down at Tristan, and see he's okay, I know you lied about him being sick just to mess with my head. That's the shit I don't like about you. There are always games. Why you gotta play games so much?"

"I'm not playing games, Claire. You're just look-ing for a reason to end the relationship and you look like you found one. You have made me out to be the bad guy and that's not fair."

Claire frowned. "Love it or leave it, but my deci-sion will still be the same."

"That's just it, I don't want to leave it anymore, Claire. You so quick to leave me when things don't go your way. People fight in relationships and it doesn't always mean that it isn't working. You're supposed to stick it out and make things work."

"Are you still seeing that nigga?"

A stick of asparagus went flying out of Bobbi's mouth when she heard the question. She coughed a few times and said, "W-what nigga?"

"The one you been fucking on the side, Bobbi. If you say you want a real relationship let's start by having real conversations. Were you or were you not already fucking that nigga before you asked me if it was cool?"

"I'm not fucking nobody, Claire. The only one I want to be with is you. I just wished you believed me. I'm not even interested in nobody else."

"That ain't what you said before," Claire reminded her.

"Well that was when I was confused, and not thinking straight. I know what I want now and I see our future clearly. Don't you want this? Don't you want your family?"

"I don't want to be in a relationship, Bobbi. I'm good on that. It's like now that I'm not with you, I realized that I'm less stressed. I'm not even sure that being with a woman is for me. I just need some space."

Bobbi was so angry she was blushing. "You think I'm stupid don't you? You actually think I believe that you not fucking with that bitch whose head I swung the other day."

"You lucky as shit, Bobbi."

141

"Please enlighten me as to why I'm so lucky."

"You lucky because if that girl would've remembered you hit her, you would've likely had a long term problem on your hands."

"Claire, I wish that chick would play me for feathery. She would be dead instead of sporting the stitches I blessed her with on the back of her scalp. Besides, if you knew who she really was you would never fuck with a chick who twerks for money. She's not an angel."

Claire frowned. "What you mean twerking for money?"

A smirk spread across Bobbi's face. "Wait...you don't know?" Bobbi said, eager to put her onto game. "That precious bitch of yours is a stripper, doll baby. She be down the strip club giving them nigga's life for a few singles. And from what I heard, she be giving them head too. Be careful where you put your lips on that chick. I heard she might have herpes."

Claire's jaw hung. She pulled it back up when she saw the look of pleasure on Bobbi's face. It wasn't like Claire was with Natalie, but she also didn't like the idea of Bobbi knowing more about Natalie's life then she did. "How you sound, Bobbi? She don't even deal with niggas. She certainly would've be fucking them for money."

Claire's response did nothing but make Bobbi angrier. Yes it was true that Bobbi put her goons onto Natalie, in an effort to find out her profile. Still, from the Intel she got nowhere in the reports did her men tell her that old girl was a full time pussy licker. Bobbi was having a hard enough time as it was keeping her part time lesbian gig with Claire. She didn't need someone who ate pussy for the love of it to come along take her away.

"So you fucking with a dyke now?" Bobbi asked. "You all the way to the left now huh? That's how you feel? I know you told me you never dealt with a female before but now I gotta wonder. So tell me, are you fucking your mother too? I mean what else don't I know about you?"

Claire got up and put the baby in the bed in his room. When she returned she got up in her face. "You trying to make me hurt you again right? Is that what you want, Bobbi?"

Bobbi backed up a little, but continued to stare Claire down. "Let me find out you fell right into that bitch's web. She a snake, Claire. A fucking snake. Don't you see that? Natalie did all she could to break us apart, and you coming at me like I'm a nigga off the street."

"That girl you talking about is my friend, and she didn't deserve to be hit over the head either."

"The bitch was eating your pussy out in my house!"

"It wasn't even like that…we were drinking and it just happened. And like I said you're lucky she didn't remember, and that I didn't have enough sense

143

to tell her what really happened, because you'd probably be in jail or dead right now."

Bobbi was enraged. "If you think I give a fuck about you telling that bitch anything you don't know me after all."

"This ignorant shit you do, with always starting drama, is the reason I don't fuck with you no more," Claire said as she turned around to approach the front door.

"Where do you think you're going?"

"Tristan is sleep so I'm leaving," she said grabbing her purse. "I'll holla at you later."

"If you leave out of that door that's it," Bobbi threatened.

"Its already over between us," she said turning the knob.

"I mean it's over for you, me *and* Tristan. Because I don't know if I told you this or not, but me and the father thinking about putting him up for adoption. If you don't help me take care of him, I'm going to take him up on the suggestion."

Claire laughed. "So let me get this straight, you talking to Vyce again?"

"Naw, he ain't the father. He never was the father. I just lied to him to get into his pockets."

Claire's mouth dropped, and her eyes widened. "So you mean to tell me, that when Vyce brought you into the house with me, that he was not the father of

144

your baby and you knew it? And you didn't even tell me?"

Bobbi grinned.

"You really are that funky and foul."

"You ain't heard foul yet, bitch," Bobbi said. "It's like this, you belong to me and there's nothing you can do about it now. You're stuck with me, and I'm stuck with you. And if I even think you are seeing Natalie again, I will sign those adoption papers so quick your head will spin, and Tristan will be placed in the system for good."

CHAPTER 20

CLAIRE

At Natalie's house...

"Claire, what is it? Just tell me," Natalie said to her as they sat on her living room sofa. "You haven't spoken to me all day and you got me worried."

"I said I don't want to talk about it," Claire said flipping the channels, as Tristan lay in the portable playpen on the floor. He was sleep. "Besides, you told me you didn't want to hear anything I had to say about Bobbi remember?"

Although Bobbi's attempt to blackmail Claire worked, it didn't mean that Claire didn't hate her. The moment Claire fell victim to her game, Bobbi got dressed, grabbed her car keys and moved for the front door. Bobbi asked her to watch Tristan so she could do God knows what and truth be told, Claire really didn't care where she went. She just wanted Bobbi to get out of her presence. Lately her mind had been going to left field and she was starting to feel crazy again. She was in over her head with all of the emotions and it didn't seem like she had a way out. Hate caused Claire to want to leave the relationship, but the love of Tristan made her want to stay.

"So you leave my house, go see Bobbi, and then come back with an attitude with me? Like I did something wrong?" Natalie responded. "I mean what the fuck did I do?"

Claire didn't understand why Natalie was getting mad. She didn't owe her an explanation. She barely wanted to give Bobbi one. Claire was seriously considering being done with everybody but there was a problem. Where would she go? She couldn't go to her mother's because she didn't bump with Humphrey. She couldn't stay with Natalie because she believed it when Bobbi said that she would give the baby up for adoption. So she had to stay with Bobbi until she could find some place safe for her and Tristan. She even thought about running away with him, but she didn't know if she was built like that and could deal with being a fugitive of the law.

"Are you a stripper?" Claire asked Natalie, getting off of the subject. "I heard something today and I want to hear it from you. Is it true?"

Natalie looked like she swallowed her whole face. "I...I use to...I mean...back in the day—"

"Why didn't you tell me? Why I had to have it thrown in my face? We're friends, Natalie, and at the very least I would hope that you'd know that you could come to me about things like this."

147

"So me and you get down like that now?" She grinned. "Because that's the only reason I didn't tell you. To be honest I thought you wouldn't care and that it didn't matter, because we weren't in a relationship."

Claire hated that Natalie looked into the matter more than what she was. So she backed up. "Me and you not doing nothing right now, but being there for each other. But, I gotta tell you it doesn't look too good. If you feel like you gotta hide stuff from me, then that's not a real friendship. "

Natalie sighed. "Like I said, yes I did use to strip a little back in the day. I needed the money and from working at the club I was able to save up a few coins and make a living for myself. When I got my desired amount, I got out of the business, bought this house and—"

"Put yourself through college," Claire said sarcastically. It was common knowledge that most strippers were putting themselves through the university that they never graduated from.

"Yes, I put myself through college." she frowned. "And I know you think it's a joke but for my case it's true. Wasn't nothing more important to me than going to college, and that's what I did."

Claire looked around her house. "So where is your degree? 'Cause from where I'm sitting I don't see it on any of your walls."

"You 'bout to eat your words, chicky," Natalie responded as she walked away.

148

Claire watched her disappear into the house. When she came back into the living room with her bachelor's degree in computer science in her hand, Claire smiled. And to really drive the matter home, Natalie also showed her the doctorate in the same field.

She handed her the degrees. "Now what, Claire?" Natalie responded placing her hands on her hips. "Are you going to continue to doubt me or understand that what I say is my bond?"

Claire looked at both of the documents. She looked up from them and asked, "Are these real?"

"Call the University of Delaware and find out for yourself if you don't believe me." She walked away with an attitude to pour herself a drink and Claire followed. "But at the end of your investigation I want an apology."

"I'm sorry, Natalie." She placed them on the table. "I just—"

"Judged me just like everybody else I know." She sipped her Merlot. "But you know what, I could take it from everybody else but I never thought I would have to take it from you. You really hurt my feelings, Claire because I never judged you once. I know stripping is not a lifestyle you can do forever. And I know it's degrading and makes the women who do it appear shallow, but just because I did that doesn't mean that being a stripper was who I was. I'm a good

149

person, and I was lucky enough to get out of the game without a drug addiction, or STD."

That was going to be Claire's second question, did she have herpes or not? She decided against asking her because she knew she was sensitive at the moment. "So were you fucking in there for money?"

"No," she said wiping her tears. "But it never mattered, I was always judged because I was on the pole. I don't wish the lifestyle on nobody, but at the time I did what I thought I had to do."

Claire was quiet. "So are you a…I mean do you only deal with—"

"Women? Yes, Claire. I'm currently not interested in men."

"Because I don't know what I am right now," she said truthfully. "When I got with Bobbi I was five seconds from marching in the gay parade. And now I'm just, well, I'm just trying to figure out what I want out of life. I use to fuck with this nigga that cheated on me with this girl at my school, and he broke my heart. I think I'm ruined mentally behind that shit."

Natalie sipped her drink. "What happened to him?"

"The same day I caught him cheating, he backed out of his driveway and a garbage truck hit his car. He was thrown from it and killed instantly." Claire looked down at her feet. "I loved him very much, and after our relationship ended, I didn't want to fall in love again. But it happened anyway when I met Vyce, and he was just as selfish."

"What was your ex-boyfriend's name? The one who was killed?"

Claire looked at her and wiped the single tear that fell from her eyes. "His name was Packs."

"Damn, I'm sorry, Claire."

"I don't know what it is about me, but I can't seem to find someone who will do me right. When me and Bobbi were fucking with Vyce, at the same time, he put us up in his house and I did everything I could to make him happy, even let him fuck another bitch in front of me, and nothing seemed to work. It's almost like people don't like you unless you treating them like shit."

"Hold fast, ya'll let a nigga post both of ya'll up in the same spot?" Natalie asked leaning closer toward her. "And ya'll didn't kill each other?"

"We both loved him," she exhaled. "At least that's what I thought I felt at the time." She paused. "What I'm trying to say is that I don't know if this gay thing is a passing moment or not, but I do know that all I want to do is spend some time getting to know me. You understand?"

"I think so," Natalie smiled.

"You mind if I go out for a second? I need to get some fresh air."

"Sure."

"Can you watch over Tristan? He's still sleeping and won't get up until way after I get back. Even if he does once you pick him up and play with him he's good."

"Claire, it's really not a problem," she smiled. "Go on out and clear your mind. I'm here for you. I told you that."

When Claire left Natalie walked over to the beautiful sleeping baby. "So it really is true, you're the one she loves the most huh?" She circled the playpen. "I wonder what she would do if I took you from this planet? She'll probably lose her mind," she laughed. "Luckily for you I'm not that cruel." She rubbed his cheek. "Well, not yet anyway."

Natalie strolled over to the phone and made a call. "Liz, it's me, Natalie." She looked at the sleeping baby again.

"What's up with you, superstar? You still selling that good pussy?"

"Shit, you know that will never change. Besides niggas pay the big bucks to get this wet-wet. And as long as it stays moist," she rubbed her hand between her legs, "that'll never change. But that ain't what I'm calling you about."

"What it do?"

"You still looking for a baby of your own?"

Liz exhaled and she tried to contain herself. "I'd give the left side of my body to have a child of my own. You know that, Natalie."

"Well luckily for you it won't be that expensive, but it will run you a few stacks and take me a few days."

"You get me a baby and you can have everything you need."

CHAPTER 21
VYCE

A t a D C public park...

Vyce watched Viva walk over to him as he sat on the park bench eating sunflower seeds. Although he fucked with all of the Lollipop Kidz, literally, she was by far his favorite. It wasn't because she was the sexiest, or better looking than the other two. But she proved that she was willing to do anything he said, and that was all he needed to put her in first place. For a woman to give him her heart and soul. And Viva looked to him as if he were God.

"Sorry I was thirty seconds late," she said kissing him on his cheek. "You not mad are you?"

"I'll get over it," he winked popping more seeds into his mouth. "But look, I need to make sure you are in agreement about what needs to happen the night of the party. We can't have any fuck ups because there will never be another chance to get them both together."

"I am willing to do anything for you, Vyce," she said passionately. "I told you that many times and in many ways."

"So what do I want you to do?" He asked. "I need to make sure you have the details down."

"You want me to help some other girls beat the shit out of Bobbi and Claire behind the museum. You want me to not stop until they can't move."

"That's, my sweet baby," he said as he spit empty shells out of his mouth, which caused one to stick to her thigh. She left it there. "You make me proud when you remember what I need you to do, and show initiative in doing it".

She smiled. "You know I'm your true soldier." Her head hung low. "But who the other girls? I kinda wanted to bring my own team to help out. Them other chicks may snitch."

He dropped the bag of sunflower seeds in his hand, stood up and gripped her throat. He squeezed so tightly he almost snapped her vocal cords. Blood rushed to the surface of her skin and caused it to redden. "What I tell you about asking me questions?"

"I'm sorry, I...I..." she cried. "I just wanted to know." She was trembling violently.

He released her and shoved her backwards. She stumbled and rubbed her neck. "Whoever I got to help is my fucking business. Now you might not like who you see when you get there, but that's just the way it is. If you can handle working with them, and if you can keep focused, then you gonna be by my side for the long haul. But I got to know that I can trust you first."

"Vyce, I don't care who you got helping me. I'm doing this shit for you. Don't worry, I can keep my cool."

He winked and sent her on her way. While he waited, had time to think. He couldn't believe all the drama he had around him these days. On top of his current situation, he had to deal with Whiz's baby's mamas shit. He couldn't believe Erica tried to shoot him the night she found out he was fucking Diane too. Out of respect for his dead homie Whiz, he decided to completely cut them off instead of killing them, especially Erica. Five minutes later, Mel and Juniper showed up looking just as raunchy as ever. His dick stiffened the moment he saw them rocking the same tight jean shorts and tighter tops that they were known for.

"Hey, my sweet daddy," Juniper grinned kissing him on the lips.

"We miss you," Mel added, rubbing his dick. She looked around. "But why we have to meet you out here?"

"Yeah, we not allowed at your house anymore?" Juniper questioned.

"You know that ain't it. This is about business, and I wanted some fresh air." He winked. "So are ya'll ready for the party that's coming up? We can't have any mistakes. I don't see another time when we will get them both together so this is it."

Juniper nodded and cracked her knuckles. "You don't have to worry about shit, we gonna murder them bitches just like we planned."

"And what if something happens?" he looked at both of them. "And you get caught by the police? Is my name going to come up?"

"We not getting caught," Mel advised with a serious expression. "We in there and when we done we out. They won't know what hit 'em. And even if they did know what hit 'em, they won't be alive to tell people what happened."

Vyce chuckled. "You talking that good shit now."

"Can I ask you something?" Juniper said twirling a strand of her hair.

He started to tell her to kick rocks like he did Viva but he was thinking about banging their backs out later and didn't want the animosity. "What?"

"Is it true you know them girls? The ones you got us taking care of?"

"I know of 'em," he admitted. "DC is kinda small."

"But you never fucked with them like that before?" she persisted.

"What I look like fucking with them classless bitches? Did you see them ratchet hoes? They not half the class acts ya'll are." He observed them in the shorts that were so tight he knew that they were baking

157

a fresh batch of yeast infection as they spoke. "Please. They not even my style."

"I told you so," Mel grinned at Juniper, eager that the rumor they heard wasn't true. "Both of them bitches are ugly and Vyce don't get down like that."

"What I want to know is are ya'll sure you're ready for the type of life I can provide you once this is all taken care of?"

"Vyce, we not about talking shit no more. We gonna show you what we ready for," Juniper added.

"Now you talking, my sweet baby! Now you're talking."

CHAPTER 22

BOBBI

I n B obbi's car...

"Ms. Ovaline, why do you keep ringing my phone back to back?" Bobbi asked as she sat in her driver's seat and smoked a blunt. Her car was parked out in front of her house. "You done called me at least five times today alone. Why not just leave a fucking message?"

"I called your phone because I told you that I wanted to talk to you yesterday, but you didn't return my call. I can be very persistent if ignored. You should know that by now."

Bobbi rolled her eyes. "Well you tricked me into answering the phone now by blocking your number, so what do you want?" she asked as she placed her feet on her dashboard. "Because the only thing I'm hearing from you now is a bunch of rattling on. Now speak quickly, I got somewhere to go later."

"I had a dream about you last night, Bobbi. You were with some other girl and both of ya'll died. I don't know what you got going on in your life, but I suggest you be very careful."

Bobbi laughed. "Ms. Ovaline, why are you having dreams about me when you don't even know me like that? Isn't that a little weird? I let you watch my baby one time when I went to see my boyfriend and now you think you my mama. Don't you have some kids of your own that you can harass?" She inhaled the smoke into her lungs and let it seep out into a cloud above her head.

Ovaline smacked her lips. "Your mama must didn't teach you any manners did she? Because you're a rude little bitch."

"My mamma did what she could but at the end of the day I'm my own woman. And can't you or nobody else tell me how to live my life. Now if you gonna tell me a dream about me dying just forget about it. Anyway like I said I'm about to go somewhere so I'll talk to you later."

"You are moving too fast, young lady. And if you hang up on me, you gonna see why they call me the Body Snatcher."

Bobbi's heart skipped a beat. She was a hot head and had a big mouth but she knew she was fucking with a thoroughbred too. "Can you just tell me this dream so I can go on about my business please?"

"Like I was saying before your rudeness, you and some other girl was crushed. I'm not sure by what 'cause I couldn't make it out. If I had to guess I'd say it was by a car or truck. Who knows? But I will say this, if I were you I would get on my knees, make

amends with everybody I've wronged in my life, and
hope that the course will be changed to prevent this
fate."

"I didn't do nobody wrong in my life," Bobbi
said, a little scared.

"Now you know I don't believe that, chile."

"You don't have to believe it."

"Bobbi, my dreams are never wrong. You cold,
real cold and it shows all over your skin."

"Once again you making judgments without
knowing me," Bobbi frowned.

"You can always tell a woman's character by the
way she treats her children, and you treat your son like
dog shit."

Bobbi was so angry she was sobbing uncontrol-
lably. She smashed the blunt out on the window and
sat up straight. "You don't know shit about me you,
fat, old bitch! Go get into somebody else's business
before I send somebody over your house to blow your
face backwards! I'm done talking to you. Eat rocks,
bitch!"

The moment she hung up on her, the phone rang
again. This time it was her cousin and Bobbi jive-like
wanted to ignore the call. But she picked it up anyway,
hoping Pookie could say something good and calm her
down. "Pookie, if you calling me on some bullshit now
is not the time."

"What the fuck is wrong with you?"

"I'm busy right now," she said wiping her tears.

161

"Don't tell me you busy, bitch, when I hear you over there crying. What the fuck is up with you? Talk to me!"

Bobbi sniffled a few times, angry that she allowed Ms. Ovaline to get her feelings off the meter. "Do you think that I'm a bad person? And before you lie please know that I want to hear the truth."

"Fuck yeah! You the baddest bitch I know!"

"I'm serious," Bobbi yelled. "Do you think I'm a bad person? Like in mean."

"I mean you not the nicest person in the world but that's what I love about you. You tell it like it is whether people want to hear it or not."

"But I don't want to be like that anymore. I want to be a person who's liked." She paused. The next question she wanted to ask was hard but she asked anyway. "Do you think I'm a bad mother?"

Pookie remained silent.

"Do you think I'm a bad mother, Pookie?" Bobbi yelled louder.

"I think you could be better."

Bobbi knew she wasn't the best but she thought she did a good job of concealing her bad side to the outer world. And now she discovered that she was wrong.

"Where is my mother?" Bobbi asked changing the subject.

"Actually she just came over here. She was talking about Tristan's party. Do you want to speak to her?" Pookie asked excitedly. They hadn't spoken in awhile and she wanted them to reconcile. Pookie was big on family. "She'd love to talk to you and see Tristan. You really should let her, Bobbi."

Bobbi thought about what Ms. Ovaline said about making amends with people in her life. Speaking to her mother was a good opportunity to expose her good side, and to show herself more than anything that she was a decent person. There was one problem though, her mother got on her fucking nerves. To make matters worse her mother put her foot down when Bobbi was living in her home. She would not tolerate her being too grown, running the streets and she would not accept Bobbi talking to her any kind of way. This is the main reason they always bumped heads.

"No, I'm good," Bobbi replied. "I got too much to do right now."

"Come on, Bobbi," Pookie begged. "Please give her a chance. The least you could do is talk to her. Wouldn't you feel bad if something happened and you never got a chance to say I love you?"

Instead of inspiring reconciliation, this did nothing but send Bobbi off the deep end. "Bitch, what the fuck you talking about if something happened? You sound dumb as shit. I'm Bobbi Gannon! I'm invincible, and you better ask some damn body about me if you don't know already!"

Pookie was silent. Although Bobbi was acting weird, she wasn't surprised. Everybody in the family knew that Bobbi could be a loose cannon. When Bobbi calmed down Pookie asked, "You done yet?"

"I guess."

"Good, because it's my turn to talk. Now you might be mad at your mother but I ain't her, bitch, and you not going to talk to me like you forgot who the fuck I be. I never did anything but stand by your side and I'm not feeling your little attitude." She paused. "Anyway you talking to your mother is not why I'm calling. I keep getting word that some girls are going to jump you and that Claire chick. You gotta be careful because something's telling me that Vyce may be involved in this shit."

"If Vyce wanted to see me he would have done it already. He certainly wouldn't send no bitches to do the job."

"What if he doesn't want to get caught? Ya'll took him for his money, Bobbi. He may be playing it smart on the revenge tip this time."

"Pookie, trust me, I know him. If anything that nigga is probably sitting up somewhere just hoping that I don't tell people what I know about the dope game he love so much. Plus he don't want nobody knowing he got ganked for his money by a couple of females. Everything will be fine."

"If you say so."

"I do."

164

CHAPTER 23

CLAIRE

In Front Of Claire's Mother's House...

Claire was walking to her car while talking on the cell phone. Claire just met with her mother to see if they could restore their relationship, but it didn't end to well because they couldn't see eye to eye about Humphrey. Things were worse when she left her mother's house, only for Bobbi to call with an attitude.

"Bobbi, I don't have time for this shit right now okay? You wanted me back home and I live there. But it doesn't mean I can't leave the house every now and again too."

"But you might as well not live here because you're never home."

Claire stopped in the driveway and sighed. "You are so fucking ridiculous. It ain't enough for you to get some of the things you want. You want everything." She looked through her purse for her car keys.

"What I want is for things to be the way they use to be between us. I feel like you don't love me no more. Like everything you do now is just to past the time or for Tristan."

165

I don't love you no more bitch. Claire thought.

Frustrated Claire said, "Can I ask you something?"

"Anything?"

"How do you want me to act, Bobbi? And don't hold back either, because its obvious that you have an idea on how I should be."

"What you mean?" Bobbi responded, not expecting her question.

"You claim I'm acting funny and shit, so how about you tell me how you would want me to act, since it's obvious I'm not doing the right things by you."

"It ain't about that."

"I'm waiting on an answer, Bobbi or else you're just wasting my time."

Bobbi smacked her lips. "I want us to be happy, but I want you to give an honest effort too. I mean, if something were to happen to me, wouldn't you feel bad for it? Wouldn't you feel terrible that you didn't do right by me? Life is short, Claire, and I just want you to realize it."

"You must need a babysitter or something," Claire responded. "That's the only reason you hitting me with this right by me shit."

"I'm serious, Claire. This ain't about no babysitter," she lied. Truth be told she was trying to hit the streets and she wanted her to come get Tristan. "I want you to be happy how you use to be when I came home. I want you to be in the house playing with Tristan, so

166

that I can come home and cook for you. I don't want something bad to happen to one of us only for you to realize that you could've tried harder."

"I'm not happy, Bobbi. You understand? You said you wanted me to live in the house, it doesn't mean I have to enjoy doing it. I got feelings you know, and I don't have them anymore for you."

"Well what about my feelings?"

"I see you're still the same selfish ass Bobbi. Only thinking about herself. The fact that you can even fix your face to come at me like that means you have zero respect for me, or our past relationship, but you know what, I'm good on that."

"There you go with that I'm good shit."

"It's the truth. I mean you said it yourself, Bobbi. Think about it for a moment. How much time have I really been putting into you lately? Zero. And you know why, because I'm done with trying to pretend that I care about you, or that you care about me. I'm just done."

"You love playing the victim," Bobbi laughed. "And you really need to understand that—"

Claire's conversation was ended when a stranger snatched the phone out of her hand. She turned around preparing to swing on whoever disrespected, until she saw *his* face and her heart stopped momentarily. Standing in front of her was the man she violated and he looked pissed.

Vyce ended the phone call and handed Claire back the phone. "How have you been, my sweet baby?" Claire was about to run until he grabbed her forcefully by the arm. "I know you're not about to run away from me just yet. We just reunited. "

Claire looked at his car and saw Tya sitting in the passenger seat. Her face looked smashed to bits but Claire knew what was going on. Tya had sold her out, and got back with Vyce. What she didn't know was that he remembered where her mother lived.

"What are you doing here?" Claire asked, trying to be strong. "And what do you want from me?"

"Now is that any way to speak to the man who you stole thousands of dollars from? If anything I should be the one angry, but I'm not."

She frowned. "Like I said what do you want with me, Vyce?"

"Believe it or not, I don't want anything. I really just stopped by to see how you were doing. And I must admit, my sweet baby, you looking good." He licked his lips. The lips at one point she loved kissing. "Really good."

"So are you going to kill me? Is this why you're here?"

"Now why would I want to hurt you?"

"You said it yourself. I stole a lot of money from you and I guess you want it back. The thing is I don't have it. I spent every last dime," she lied.

168

"The only thing I want to know from you is one question. Just one. Is Bobbi's pussy still sweet?"

"I don't know what you're talking about," she responded shuffling where she stood. "I haven't spoken to Bobbi since we left your house. Why would you even come at me like that?"

"Sure you know where she is. Everybody in DC knows what you two have been doing behind closed doors. So there's really no reason to lie to me, Claire. Is her pussy sweet or not?"

Maybe it was the fact that Claire had grown since he last saw her, or maybe it was the fact that she wanted him to know that he could no longer hurt her. But for some reason she was emboldened and decided to tell him straight to his face how she felt about him.

Claire approached him slowly. She was so close to him that at first he thought she was about to kiss him again. In his warped mind he actually believed that she still had feelings for him.

Until with a sly grin on her face she said, "You wouldn't begin to understand how juicy her pussy is. Especially since we both stopped stuffing it with dick. *Your dick.* The best thing we could've done was leaving you and that trash penis that sadly enough, you're stuck with. So to answer your question yes, her pussy is not only sweet, but sweeter since she stopped giving it to you."

The smile was removed from his face. He was just about to lay hands on her for insulting his manhood when her mother opened the front door. "Claire, is everything okay out there?"

Claire looked at her mother and then back at Vyce, who jumped in his car and pulled off. She wasn't certain but she had a feeling that her mother just saved her life.

"Everything is okay now, ma." She smiled. Her heart beat rapidly.

"Well come back inside. I don't trust what I just saw."

CHAPTER 24

BOBBI

I n B obbi and C laire's living room...

Claire paced the living room carpet as she re-called how close she believed she came to death. But when Claire told Bobbi what happened at her mother's house, with Vyce, as usual Bobbi annoyed her by be-lieving that she was overreacting.

"What you need to do is calm down," Bobbi said to Claire as they sat on the living room sofa. "If the nigga wanted you dead you'd be dead right now. Vyce would not have hesitated to take care of you. If any-thing it means what I think, that Vyce knows he owed us the money and he's backing off. He doesn't want the drama."

Claire stood up. "Bitch, did you just say calm down? Do you realize that the man we took for about a half a million dollars came at me today? He was live and in the flesh, Bobbi. It wasn't a game. The only reason he didn't push off was because my mother was there."

"And yet you survived, Claire," Bobbi said calm-ly.

"I can't believe you acting like this shit wasn't a big deal. This nigga stepped to me and if he wanted to all he had to do was pull the trigger and I would be dead right now. We can't go back to DC, Bobbi. I don't feel like it's safe anymore. Maybe you should change Tristan's party and have it in Delaware instead. Something doesn't feel right."

Bobbi shook her head and leaned back into the sofa. "I'm not doing that shit."

"Why the fuck not?"

"Well I have several reasons," she responded rolling her eyes. "Which one do you want?"

"All I need is one GOOD reason on why you still think it's cool to have your only son's party in a city where someone we wronged is trying to kill us."

"I'll give you several reasons. First of all my peoples live in DC, and ain't nobody driving way up here, in Delaware, for my baby's party. Secondly, all his friends are out DC too. I want him to enjoy himself, Claire. I don't want him to be worried about a man who might or might not do something to his mother. It's a waste of my energy and time, and I'm paying Vyce no fucking attention."

Claire shook her head in disbelief. "Do you realize how stupid you sound right now? I just told you that a nigga wanted to kill me, and the only thing you thinking about is a party. I didn't even tell you this, but Tya was in the car with him. Her face was beaten and everything." Bobbi looked a little frightened hearing

172

that news. "We better hope he doesn't tie her ass up and make her tell us where we live," Claire continued.

"Claire, if Tya remembered where we lived, and if you are right about Vyce wanting to kill us, he would've been here by now. Like I said you need to relax, and let's not cancel Tristan's party over nothing. That's all I'm saying."

"All you want to do is show off for your fake ass friends and family, and let everybody see the big party you're giving Tristan. I hate that you are not the person I thought you were. I hate that you don't think about anybody but yourself, and I hate that Tristan has you for a mother."

Since it marked the second time in a week somebody labeled Bobbi as a bad mother her stomached cramped up. She sat back on the sofa and rubbed it softly. In a voice that was barely audible Bobbi replied, "But I don't know how to change, Claire." She looked at her with soft eyes. "Where do I start?"

"What?" Claire screamed, unable to hear her. "Open your fucking mouth. I can't hear what you're saying."

Claire had no idea that in that moment, Bobbi was trying to reach out for help. Claire was so use to her being strong and loud, that she didn't even know it was possible for Bobbi to be any other way.

Instead of allowing the moment of vulnerability to takeover, which would show Claire her gentler side, Bobbi went Southeast DC again. "You don't know what the fuck you talking about," she said loudly. "I'm a way better mother than you are, I do know that much."

"You must be out of your mind if you think you're a better mother than me, and I do know exactly what I'm talking about. Let us not forget that I'm the one who witnessed you snatching the baby out of my hands just because he didn't like you."

Bobbi was so angry her fist was balled up and sweat poured down her face. "You mean just because you turned him against me. Because that's what really happened."

Claire laughed. "How does one turn a baby against you? Huh? He's a baby, Bobbi. All you gotta do is like him and you can't even do that. Whenever you in his presence you passing him off to anybody with a lap so that you don't have to watch him, and then you expect him to know you. Like I said you are an awful fucking mother."

Through slanted eyes she said, "You are so high and mighty. Have you forgotten that you killed a person? I don't recall murderers getting the mother of the year award either."

Hearing her crime out loud, made Claire wonder if she could trust her not to go to the cops. "It ain't about being high and mighty, and let us not forget that I committed that crime for you. For both of us. Had I not pulled that trigger Whiz may have told Vyce what we were doing, and he would've gotten both of us."

"You can try and convince yourself of that if you want to, but me and you both know the truth." She grinned. "It's a good thing that Vyce didn't come see me before he saw you. I may have told him about what happened to his best friend, and he would've really wanted you dead then."

Claire's heart beat wildly. "You would do that dirty shit wouldn't you?"

"Maybe, or maybe not. It depends on how I feel later about you claiming I'm not a good mother. Which is crazy considering I was able to give birth to a son."

Claire knew she was trying to hurt her emotionally for not being able to have a baby but she kept it together. "Having a son don't make you no mother," Claire responded, as she walked away to grab her purse.

"She who doesn't have a son and can't have one should remain silent."

Claire stopped in place and looked at Bobbi. "You can't hurt me with that shit no more, Bobbi. I'm quite aware that I can't give birth and may never be able to. But guess what, with all that said it still doesn't mean that you are a better mother than me." Tears rolled down her eyes and she allowed them to fall. "I love that little boy in that room, and if you try to keep me from him you gonna have a problem on your hands. And in case you think it's a game, don't forget that like you said, I have killed once, and I don't

175

have any problems killing again. It would take your family months just to find your teeth to bury for a funeral. Be careful, Bobbi. Really careful."

Bobbi bit down on her bottom lip. It was as if they were playing mental Chess and Bobbi's life depended upon the next move. She thought about what Claire represented...stability and financial security. Bobbi knew that she didn't want to be in a relationship per say, but she needed Claire if she was going to have her freedom. And if she gave the baby up for adoption, she doubted that she would be able to live with herself, and the finger pointing from her family. So she had to be cool.

"I would never keep you away from Tristan." Claire was shocked at her response. "But you need to know this too, I'm having his birthday party at the museum. Call me dumb if you want to, but I'm not going to allow Vyce's crazy ass to stop him from having his day."

"And I'm begging you to reconsider, Bobbi. I don't think it's safe."

"I gave you my answer already, Claire. The only thing you should be asking yourself now is if you are still coming or not."

"So there ain't nothing I can say to get you to change your mind?"

"Nothing."

Claire wiped the tears from her face. "Well, for Tristan I'll do anything. But you do need to know that you and me are officially over, and I'm moving out tonight."

"Do what you gotta do."

CHAPTER 25

CLAIRE

A t the museum in W ashington D C

Claire was sitting on one of the chairs in the party room at the museum. Bobbi was right, everything was beautiful and it looked like they were having a celebration for the child of a star. The employees at the museum tended to their every need while others who dressed up like dinosaurs played with the children.

Tristan was sitting on Claire's lap and looking into her eyes while the party and chaos went on around them.

Claire didn't feel guilty for stealing him away from the festivities, because every time Claire moved Tristan kept chasing behind her, wanting her attention. Not to mention the fact that Tristan didn't get along with any of the kids in the room. They were too mean, too loud, and violent or too sick, and Claire didn't want her baby around any of the nonsense.

Briefly she looked out into the party to see where Bobbi was, and as usual she was nowhere to be found. It was fine with Claire because she didn't want to see Bobbi anyway.

"I love you, Tristan," she said softly stroking his curly hair backwards. "You don't have to worry about anything as long as I'm alive, because I love you so much, and I will always take care of you. I will kill somebody if they tried to take you away from me."

He laughed and tugged her bottom lip before pulling it roughly like most babies do when they get a good grip. They were in their own world until Pookie walked over to Claire with a major attitude. Like somebody pissed in her lap or something.

"Uh...so you gonna just roughhouse the baby all night?" she asked with her hands on her hips. "Act like this ain't his party and ya'll somewhere alone?"

"Roughhouse the baby?" she repeated. "What you talking about, Pookie? I don't have no time for this shit." Claire focused on Tristan again who didn't seem bothered by his second cousin's rudeness.

"It's Tristan's birthday party, yet you over here with him by yourself. His family does want to see him you know?"

"First off you were over there getting your ass kicked in Spades," Claire said calmly not trying to frighten Tristan. "And second of all he has been over here with me for about thirty minutes and not one of these kids in here gives a fuck. This party ain't about Tristan, it's about ya'll and trying to make yourself look good. But luckily since I helped pay for this event, I can do what I want."

Pookie's face was as hard as stone. "You not his mother you know?"

Boy was Claire getting tired of hearing that shit. She felt like schooling old girl on what being a mother was, like she had Bobbi, but today was Tristan's day not hers. "And your point is?"

"And my point is that he's blood to me. To you he ain't shit. And you need to know something else too. Bobbi may be with that shit ya'll be doing under the covers, but I'm not. The bible says—"

"Pookie, don't come over here with the Bible says shit," she said putting her hand in her face. "The bible also talks about lying, judging people, eating shellfish and a whole bunch of stuff but it never seems to stop people picking and choosing what they want to say about the bible."

"Well I want you to leave my cousin alone," Pookie continued, not having a better point. "Because I'm gonna put a stop to this relationship ya'll have if it's the last thing I do." Claire laughed and this pissed Pookie off even more. "What the fuck is so funny?"

"I'm laughing at you, clown! You over here talking to me about what your cousin and me did or do in the bedroom when it ain't your place. If folks spent more time worrying about how clean their own sheets are instead of poking their noses into other people's bedrooms the world would be a nicer place." She sat Tristan down and stood up so that she was staring directly into her eyes. "Now what you need to know is this, who I'm fucking, and how I'm fucking them don't have shit to do with you. And that goes for whatever I plan on doing with your cousin too." Claire knew she could've told her they were broken up, but she chose not to. "If you forget that again, I ain't got no problem giving you a reminder."

When Pookie looked around everybody was staring at them. Embarrassed that Claire had assembled and audience, most of which consisted of her nosey cousins who would never let her live this situation down if Claire got out on her, Pookie hit her in the face.

Claire beat her ass until her real nails came off.

CHAPTER 26

BOBBI

In Red's car outside of the party...

Bobbi was confused on what was going on from the passenger seat of Red's car. She watched her ex-girlfriend be carried out of Tristan's party by the cops, in handcuffs, while her cousin was rolled out on a stretcher. Instead of celebrating the baby's birthday, at the party she just had to have, she was outside of the museum, sitting in the car with Red smoking a J.

"Red, I gotta go see what's going on," her eyes spread widely. "You see that shit?"

He frowned, and looked around the car. "Well hurry up back. We gotta finish talking."

Bobbi hopped out of the car and rushed toward the museums entrance. She stomped up to a pile of her cousins who were just talking about the event in the middle of the floor. "Shane, what just happened? Why the cops here and why they take Claire?"

Shane rolled her eyes. "What didn't happen? For starters that girl you had watching Tristan beat on

Pookie's face like a drum. Girl it took me, five of our older cousins and your mother to pull her off."

Bobbi's mouth dropped. "What you talking about? Why would Claire beat on her?"

"I don't know," she shrugged, "but your mother is over there with Tristan now. Go talk to her." She pointed behind Bobbi. "Tristan was upset when they started fighting and shit too. He kept yelling Claire's name. The shit was so sad, girl. That little boy loves her."

Bobbi didn't feel like dealing with her mother but she knew she had to get it over with. So she walked toward her mother who was playing with Tristan in her lap. "Hey, ma," Bobbi said stuffing her hands into her jean pockets. "Everything cool?"

Felicia looked up at her daughter and smiled. "Hey, baby." She looked back at her grandson. "Tristan really is beautiful, Bobbi. And he's such a good baby. He stopped crying the moment I picked him up. You did good with him. Really good."

Bobbi smiled although she knew she didn't deserve the credit. Claire was the reason Tristan was well taken care of. In an effort to make calm conversation she said, "Thanks, ma. He's getting big too. Eating me out of house and home and everything."

Felicia exhaled. "Bobbi, I know this is the wrong place so I won't say too much right now."

"Ma, I don't feel like fighting with you."

183

"It won't be a fight," she said softly. "All I want to tell you is that your life is your life, and I will no longer try to stand in your way. Yes I will always be here when you need me, but I also understand that I have to allow you to do you. It took a long time getting to the realization but it's true. I love you, and you're an adult now. So I have to let you run your family."

Once again a pivotal moment occurred in Bobbi's life. She battled with whether to tell her mother that she loved her also, and that she missed her even though her actions didn't speak on it. But the hardened part of Bobbi that needed to be evil to protect her feelings, wouldn't allow her to release the pain.

"That's cool, ma," she said. "Glad you could finally see things my way."

Felicia frowned. "I said I love you, and the only thing you tell me is it's cool?"

"Well if you really love me it shouldn't matter if I say it back or not right?" When her phone rang in her pocket, she walked off without saying goodbye to her mother. "Hello."

"Baby, where you at?" Red asked. "You got me out here geeking and shit. We didn't even finish talking and fooling around yet. Come back out, Bobbi. I miss you."

Bobbi smiled. "Sorry, baby. You know I had to find out what was going on at the party. A lot of shit just kicked off in here."

"Well come around to the back of the museum. I'm in my car. I want to tap those goods before I let you go do your thing."

Bobbi grinned and said, "I'm on my way."

CHAPTER 27

BOBBI

I n the back of the museum...

Bobbi was in Red's car riding his dick in the backseat. He was giving her long strokes and every fiber of her being tingled. Sweat poured off of her face and the inside of his car was so foggy that they couldn't see outside.

"You know this is wrong right," Bobbi whispered before kissing him on the lips. "So wrong."

Red gripped at her ass cheeks and said, "Anything this good can't be wrong. What you talking about?"

Bobbi continued to enjoy their session. "You know it's bad that me and you out here fucking, when our son is in there at his party alone. You made me ditch my entire family, plus I don't even know how Pookie is doing."

"I thought your cousin Shane said she just needed a few stitches," he continued fucking her harder. "You don't have to be there for all of that. You with me, and we enjoying each other's time."

"I know, but I still feel bad," she said as she bit down on her bottom lip and moved her hips widely. "And I feel so good too."

"Naw, I'm going to tell you what's wrong in a minute," he said before he released his nut into her body.

"I know you didn't cum that quick," she said slapping his shoulder as she looked down at him. "You knew I was about to get mine too. Why you ain't hold out a little longer, Red, dang?" she said with an attitude. The two minute brother shit annoyed her sometimes. "Now what were you talking about being wrong?" she asked as she eased into the passenger seat to pull up her pants. "Cause you talking in circles now."

"What's wrong is that you was trying to take me to court for child support when you said you wouldn't do that," he said looking over at her. "What's up with that?"

Not only did Bobbi have no idea what he was talking about, but he also looked like a monster. He no longer looked like the man she was sexing just a moment ago. Instead He resembled a crazed maniac and the air in the car felt thicker.

"Red, what are you talking about? I'm confused right now." she zipped her jeans and pulled down her shirt. "I never was going to take you to no child—"

Her statement was shortened when he stole her in the mouth like she was a dude off the street. She cov-

187

ered her bloodied lips and her eyes widened. Red had never done anything like that before and she was frightened. Why was this happening all of a sudden?

"Don't lie, bitch! I know you were going to take me to child support because I got this in the mail."

He whipped a document out, and Bobbi eyed it. It was obvious that the envelope had been handwritten and it was sloppy. The writing was shoddy at best. She couldn't believe he thought that the document he was holding was official.

"Red," she said carefully, "baby, I didn't go to no fucking child support office." She took the document from him and flipped it over. "I would never do that to you. Look at this shit, baby. It's a fake!"

"But you did do it to me," he screamed in her face, causing her eyelashes to flutter. "You went down there and told them people on me. You won't be happy until you get a nigga's money, well you not getting mine. Do you hear me? You not getting mine!"

Bobbi had no idea, because Red didn't know either, that Vyce went through such lengths to fuck with her mind by forging a child support document. Vyce discovered with Viva's help that Red got rid of a girl name Nikki Jakes, a chick he got pregnant five years ago for fear that she would take him to child support court. They hadn't found her body since. Sure Vyce could've killed Bobbi and Claire himself, but it wasn't about that for him. He wanted to make them suffer, to bring down their worlds slowly like they had his. And in Bobbi's case so far it was working.

"Red, I don't know what's going on but I didn't do this to you. I would never hurt you like this. You gotta believe me."

When Red beeped his horn she had no idea what was going on, until her car door opened and she was dragged out of it by her hair. Someone yanked her like she was a bag of trash.

"Get off of me," she screamed, not knowing who had her and why. "Get the fuck off of me!"

They pulled her so far down the parking lot that her skin on her back was peeled off and her face was bloodied as feet came down on her body with extreme force.

"Talk that shit now," Juniper said. "We heard what the fuck you been saying about us."

Bobbi tried to back away, but Mel rushed up to her and hit her in the middle of the face with the bat. "Naw, bitch, you not going nowhere," Mel yelled. "Why you lie huh? Why you tell niggas me and my cousin Juniper got HIV?" she hit her again. "Why you putting them lies out there like that?"

Although Bobbi was in pain, she was also beyond confused. She didn't even know them let alone spread vicious lies on them. When she looked down the parking lot to see where Red was she noticed he pulled off. He had set her up to be jumped and he didn't even care about her well-being, or if she would

189

survive. She wasted all of her time with him, only for him to prove over and over who he really was…a bum. A selfish ass nigga. If only she listened to Claire this wouldn't be happening, but now it was too late.

"Please hear me out," Bobbi responded weakly, "whoever said I said anything about ya'll lied." She spit a tooth out of her mouth and she saw stars. "I don't even know ya'll so why would I do that? What would I have to gain?"

When she was kicked in the back of the head she saw another girl. "Shut up, bitch. We not trying to hear you say nothing."

Bobbi looked up at her, and could not recognize her face either.

"So you didn't lie about me fucking this dude name Bird Reynolds either huh?" Viva asked. "Is that what you saying to my face?"

Although Bobbi was beaten up she finally realized what was going on. Vyce had done a superb job of messing up her life. He orchestrated the entire thing and it was going down in his favor. Although she was fucked up it wasn't over yet. She had talked her way out of a beat down before and she could do it again.

"Before ya'll do anything else please listen to me. If I'm right all of this is about Vyce." The look in their eyes told her she was correct. "The nigga lied to all of ya'll. I don't know what he told ya'll but I use to fuck with him back in the day. The nigga put me up in his house with my friend, and did us wrong so we took him for his paper. If ya'll don't get away from him he'll do the same thing to you too." She wiped the blood off of her face. "He'll tear your friendships up and have ya'll fighting each other in the end. Please don't do this. Don't let him make ya'll fight his battle."

Secretly the Lollipop Kidz knew she was right but Vyce was just too good. He whined them, dined them and told them everything they wanted to hear. In the end, they gave him their souls.

"Bitch, you don't know nothing 'bout us," Viva said. "Vyce loves us, and he wouldn't lie to us especially for nobody like you. He took care of me when nobody else did. And even if he did lie you must've did something to deserve it."

Not wanting to hear another word, they presented Bobbi with the assault of her life. And when she looked to the left, up the parking lot, in the red car that had been there all along, she saw Vyce who winked at her.

191

CHAPTER 28

CLAIRE

In C laire and B obbi's home in D elaware...

Claire had been in bed for the past two days after hearing the news that Bobbi was murdered. Although everybody who knew about the situation was aware that Claire was locked up for beating on Pookie, an ugly rumor had spread its legs that the fight she had with Pookie was a distraction. In other words they were saying that Claire started the fight at Tristan's party, just to have Bobbi lured outside and murdered and it ripped her heart because it was untrue.

Claire was sitting in jail when she learned later that night that Bobbi was beat to death in the parking lot, but she didn't get a chance to grieve when she learned that people said that she was involved. No matter how much Claire denied the accusation some people just chose not to believe her. She had no idea that Vyce was up to his old tricks again.

"Can I get you anything else, baby," Natalie said as she walked into the room with a cup of steaming hot peach tea.

"I just want to be left alone," Claire admitted. "I can't believe...I mean...I still can't believe they did her like that. They beat her outside in broad daylight and nobody knows nothing." She wiped her tears. "They don't even give a fuck."

Natalie sat the cup on the table by the bed. Although Claire was an emotional wreck, Natalie was caught smiling. When Claire asked why she had a grin on her face, Natalie was able to think quickly on her feet. She told her that although the situation was horrible, she was smiling because Claire was still alive. She said that had she not been with Pookie, somebody could've jumped her too and they both would be dead. The truth was Bobbi getting beat up and murdered the way that she had was an early Christmas present for Natalie, and she couldn't contain herself or hide her joy.

"I know, Claire"— Natalie sat on the edge of the bed— "although Bobbi and I had our differences I can't imagine her being done so badly. Do they know who did it yet?"

"The last I heard no, but the family is not talking to me," Claire said blowing her nose. "The only thing they want is for me to give Tristan back, and I'm not doing that."

This pissed Natalie off because she wanted both the baby and Bobbi out of Claire's life for good. She got half of her gift with Bobbi being gone but not the other half, the most important half. "Maybe you should

193

give him back, Claire. I mean they are his family, and they deserve to be around him."

"If Bobbi had wanted them to have custody she would've written it in the letter she gave Mrs. Ovaline."

"How do you know that letter wasn't a fraud?"

"Because I know Bobbi's handwriting. She gave Ovaline the letter before she went to the party. She said if anything ever happened to her, then she wanted me to have the letter. Bobbi wants Tristan to grow up with me because she knows that I love him, and I'm not giving him up. I'm going to raise him until he's grown and that's on everything I love."

"I'm not trying to make you upset, Claire. I know that you know that I'm in your corner. It's just that this has been so hard for you. I hate to think about the drama they'll cause if you don't give them Tristan. Just let him go with them."

Claire blew her nose into the tissue and tossed it on the floor. "Natalie, I want you out of my fucking house."

Her eyes widened and her feelings were hurt. "What? Why, baby?"

"Because I told you how I feel when it comes to Tristan. I don't care who has something to say about it. When it comes to that little boy in that other room I'm sold. He will always be in my life and I will always be in his. And if the law has something to say about it they can see me too."

"I wasn't trying to—"

"I want you out, Natalie!"

"Claire, please don't do this," she said softly. "I mean, I know I come out of my mouth fast sometimes but you have to remember something, I'm in your corner. But it's like if your mother or me are not saying the things that you want to hear you cast us out of your life. Only fake bitches keep shit part-time. I keep shit real with you all of the time, because I would want the same thing in return. Yes my delivery could've been a little different but don't hate me for that. I care about you, Claire."

As much as Claire hated to admit it, Natalie sure did know how to talk some good shit. If Claire were aware of Natalie's life as a prostitute she would understand why she could talk so smoothly. She did it for a living.

"Can you give me a few moments alone please?" Claire asked her. "I just need to be alone with my thoughts. I think I'm losing my mind and I don't want to do that."

"Sure, Claire," Natalie responded, "you take some moments alone and I'll go to Tristan's room and check on him."

When Natalie left Claire pulled the sheets over top of her head and closed her eyes tightly. She took a deep breath and said, "Packs, I know you said you were not going to bother me again, but I need you right now. Please tell me what to do."

195

When she opened her eyes he was under the sheets with her. Claire was going off of the deep in now. Psychologically she was a mess and she needed help. The more pressure she was exposed to, the worse her mental stability became. "Hey, baby," he smiled. "Glad you called on me."

Although Claire was all right most days, what she didn't tell people was that she sometimes saw people who weren't there. She managed to keep her illness a secret when things were going regular, which is why she always tried to avoid drama and wanted to leave Bobbi alone. But when she was too excited, or too worried about the future, she would see extra toes on her feet or even extra fingers on her hands. But the eeriest thing she would see was people, especially her ex-boyfriend Packs who died a while back in front of her.

"I don't feel good, Packs," Claire said. "I don't know what to do. Everything is so confusing."

"Then come with me," he said softly. "I see the anti-depression medicine you got on the dresser next to you. Take the entire bottle and come with me. It's so much better on my side, babes."

Not only was Packs dangerous because he wasn't really there, but she only saw him when she was extremely sad or depressed. Secretly she missed him deep down inside, and never got over how he treated her before he died. So she was always looking for someone to fulfill what she missed about him.

196

"I'm not ready right now, Packs. I have Tristan and he needs me."

Packs frowned. "Then what you call on me for?"

"For advice. I don't know what to do. Should I give the baby up to his family or—"

"The kid loves you," he said dryly. "And you know that was hard for me to say but it's true. If you give up on him now, he won't have anybody in his corner. But if you do let him go, you can take your life and come with me. You know I'm always waiting."

Claire closed her eyes tightly and said, "Bye, Packs." When she opened her eyes he was gone, and her phone rang.

She answered it although she didn't want to talk to anyone. It was her mother but she'd been dodging her ever since Bobbi died and she needed to speak to her and get it over with.

"Hello, ma. What's up?"

"Claire, I need to see you right away, something came up."

****

"Mama, how do you know it was him?" Claire asked as she sat on the barstool in her mother's kitchen. "I thought you said you didn't see his face clearly."

"Because I know it was him," Ricky said. "And ain't no need in you asking me if I'm crazy because I know I'm not. That Vyce boy was out in front of my hair salon, just staring at me and cracking his knuckles. What the fuck happened when you two were together, Claire? I need to understand why he's being so crazy years later. "

Claire couldn't tell her mother that she robbed him because she'd never hear the last of it. Although she did her dirt she preferred when her mother wasn't around. "He just mad cause I ain't want him no more, ma. I told you that."

"Well it seems—"

When a brick came flying into the kitchen window it startled them. Claire and Ricky hit the kitchen floor wondering what was going on. When Ricky raised her head she could see Vyce outside with a lot of men.

"Ricky, just send Claire out here for a minute," Vyce yelled, "All I want to do is talk to her. We got some business that needs handling. Just the two of us."

From the floor Claire looked at her mother. She felt terrible for putting her in the predicament but there was nothing she could do, but go see what he wanted. "Ma, let me go out there, please, I don't want this around your house."

"Fuck no," Ricky said grabbing her arm. "I know what to do." She paused. "Tell him you'll be out soon."

Claire remained on the floor. "Vyce, give me a second I'll be out in a minute," she yelled.

"Good, and don't think about calling the police, unless you want something to happen to that little boy you be falling all over. What's his name? The one ya'll tried to pass off as my son? Yeah that's right, Tristan?"

Claire's heart dropped.

Hearing Tristan's name caused her to go into hysterics. Ricky placed her hands on her baby's face and looked into her eyes. "Claire, pull your mothafuckin' self together. You with me now and I'm never going to let anybody hurt you again. Do you hear me?" Ricky wiped the tears from her face. "You were right the last time I saw you. I had a duty to protect you when you were a child and I didn't. I will never let that happen again. I will always protect you and this means from your father, and that nigga outside right now. Do you hear me?"

Claire nodded.

Ricky crawled toward the phone and made a call. Since the person she was dialing didn't answer she left a message. Ten minutes later Ricky received a return call. She smiled and stood up. "Get up, Claire." She reached for her daughter's hand. "It's time to handle business."

"But I don't want you going out there, ma. Vyce is crazy and stupid. And I know he had something to do with Bobbi being murdered. If we walk out he'll kill us too."

"It's cool," Ricky smiled calmly, "trust me."

199

The moment she stood up and walked toward the door, Claire saw at least fifteen motorcycles pull up behind Vyce and his men. The riders got off of their bikes and Vyce's men aimed their guns at them. When Claire squinted to see who the bikers were she saw that one of them was Humphrey, Ricky's boyfriend.

Claire and Ricky stood next to the door. Because Humphrey didn't want them walking any further.

"I understand you got a question for my step-daughter?" Humphrey asked Vyce walking directly into his breathing space. "Well consider me her representation, nigga. Give me the message."

Vyce grinned and looked into his eyes. Although he knew the police wouldn't be called because of Tristan, he certainly didn't expect that Claire would have access to so much manpower. There were twenty men to Vyce's ten, and they were clearly outnumbered.

"Who are you?" Vyce asked Humphrey.

"Nigga, you on my property, fucking with my family. You don't get to ask me shit. The question is who the fuck are you?"

"You got it, baby boy," Vyce said. Vyce threw his hands up in the air to surrender. But the move caused all of Humphrey's men to cock their weapons, which resulted in Vyce getting filled up with led if he bucked. Luckily for him they were easy.

"It's not a problem, I'm out," Vyce said opening his car door. He eyed Claire who was hugging her mother in the doorway. "But Claire needs to know that I will be back. We have business to discuss."

"And when you do have a conversation with her, we'll be with her too," Humphrey replied.

"You can't always protect her, man. Even dogs gotta sleep."

"Watch me."

Vyce and his men piled into their cars and pulled off. Humphrey and his biker crew hung behind to make sure they were all off the property. When Claire felt a vibration in her pocket, she removed the phone remembering that Vyce brought up Tristan's name. It was Natalie.

"Claire, it's me," Natalie sobbed. "It's about Tristan. He's gone!"

Claire fainted.

EPILOGUE

Claire was exhausted after Bobbi's funeral and her body was placed in the ground. At first she wasn't going to go, but true to Humphrey's word, he and his men were there in their smelly motorcycle biker jackets and jeans. They came armed with bottles of liquor and cans of beer but at least she felt safe and was able to attend the service with them having her back.

Ever since Claire learned that Vyce took Tristan, she lost her mind. Now she felt selfish for not giving him to Pookie and the family when they asked her. Because had she done that, at least he would be safe and with his own blood.

Natalie told her she was using the bathroom, and when she went to check on Tristan, the window was broken and Tristan was gone.

She was about to get into the town car with her mother when Bobbi's mother Felicia walked up to her. Her face was as hard as stone and her eyes were narrow. Claire knew immediately that she was no nonsense and meant business.

"Is it true?" Felicia asked Claire. "That you lured my daughter to her death?"

Claire exhaled. "No, ma'am, I begged her not to have that party in DC," she responded wiping her tears. "But she wouldn't listen to me. She kept saying that all of Tristan's friends were there."

Felicia sighed. "I believe you." She looked at the ground.

Since everybody else in Bobbi's family didn't believe Claire, she was able to breathe a slight sigh of relief hearing the kind words from her mother. "Thank you," Claire replied. "For believing me."

Felicia looked behind Claire. "Where is my grandson?"

Claire swallowed and immediately seemed guilty. "He's home."

"Home? Why wouldn't you allow him to see his mother being buried, Claire? That little boy will hate you for this. Trust me."

"I didn't want him seeing nothing like this because he's too young," she lied.

The motorcycles revved up in the background to let the old woman know that it was time for Claire to bounce, and that Claire had protection. "I don't believe you, Claire. Something has happened to my baby, hasn't it? Where...is...he?"

"I'm being h-honest," Claire stuttered. "he's at home. There's too much going on and I didn't want him here. Like I said."

"When can we see him?"

"When the time is right."

"I hope you know that I'm not going to allow you to keep him from us forever, Claire. I laid my eyes on that baby once and he stole my heart. I take that very

203

*seriously and I will fight you with everything I have.
He belongs to us. He belongs to his family."*

"You do what you gotta do," Claire responded.

*"I intend too," she said walking away, and into
the arms of Pookie who was staring Claire down.*

*Pookie didn't show her ass because her aunt Fe-
licia begged her not to at the funeral, but she was just
itching for round two with Claire since everybody said
Claire won the fight.*

*After the funeral Claire went home to Natalie. A
couple of bikers posted outside of her home in Delaware, and they were loud, rude and drank too much
liquor, but she knew with them she was safe. She also
wasn't naive. She knew the moment her mother got
into an argument with Humphrey, like she did all of
her men, the guards would be called off and she would
be alone. So she needed to come up with a plan to protect herself and Natalie.*

*"How was the funeral?" Natalie asked handing
her a glass of wine. She'd already gave beers to the
bikers outside of the house who were protecting them.*

"Terrible, Natalie."

*"I was just reading something in the paper," she
showed her. "Don't you know this girl Tya Lloyd?"*

*Claire took the paper out of her hand and read
the headline. She sighed. Tya, who she last saw in
Vyce's car was murdered and she knew he did it. Her
body was found in the yard behind her mother's house.
Vyce was so disrespectful.*

"This is bad. Really bad." She threw it on the floor.

"Can I do anything for you?"

"Yeah, can you get me the baby back?" Claire asked her. "Can you tell me how to get Tristan back without getting myself killed?"

"I wish I could, Claire."

"I know you can't," Claire sighed. "I'm just venting"— she drank all of the wine and placed the glass down on the table— "Now I wish I would've gave him to this family, you know. Because I know Felicia not going to stop until she finds him. And whoever is involved she's going to have murdered. I'm not going to be able to keep saying she can't see him. I gotta meet Vyce and get this shit over with."

"You would've given him up for real?" Natalie asked. "Back to his family?"

"In a heartbeat, but I guess it don't matter anymore." She walked away. "I gotta meet with Vyce and make some sort of arrangement. Whatever happens to me I deserve anyway."

When Claire disappeared into the house, Natalie got on the phone. When Natalie sold the baby to Liz it was only because she thought that Claire wouldn't be interested in letting him go. Things worked out when Natalie found out that Vyce used Tristan's name at Claire's mother's house. It was the perfect timing because Natalie was able to let Claire think that Vyce was involved. The only problem was if Claire called

205

Vyce and agreed to meet with him, in exchange for the baby that he doesn't have, things could backfire on Natalie. Because she knew that Vyce didn't have the baby, but that she did. Claire's life was on the line and Natalie wanted the baby boy back.

She walked into the basement to continue her call. "Liz, how is the baby?"

"He's beautiful, Natalie," she boasted. "And playful too."

"Good, because I'm going to need for you to give him back to me. I'm sorry."

"I'm afraid I can't do that."

Natalie frowned. "I'm sorry that I didn't clarify the situation. You don't have a choice. I'll be over there tomorrow to get the baby. Have him ready."

****

The Lollipop Kidz were sitting on the porch with tight faces and stinky pussies. Ever since they murdered Bobbi Gannon for Vyce, he ignored them. He wouldn't answer their phone calls and he disregarded all of the messages they gave his friends to call them back.

"You know the girl we banked was right," Viva said looking at Juniper and Mel.

Mel sighed. "I know, he played us after he got what he wanted."

"So what we gonna do?" Juniper asked.

"I got the bat that Vyce gave me to use on her," Viva responded.

"So what's your point?" Mel questioned.

"It was the same bat ya'll used to break that chick's windows out. I wore gloves when I used it on Bobbi, but it has Vyce's fingerprints on it along with Bobbi's blood," Viva responded.

"So we taking it to the cops?" Mel grinned.

"You know it," Viva said. "Since he wanna run game, it's going to cost him."

THE COMPLETE NOVEL.
FROM THE BOOK '*SOFT*'

LUXURY TAX

THE COMPLETE SERIES

T. STYLES

NATIONAL BESTSELLING AUTHOR OF *RAUNCHY*

CARTEL PUBLICATIONS
PRESENTS

The Cartel Collection
Established in January 2008
We're growing stronger by the month!!!
www.thecartelpublications.com

Cartel Publications Order Form
Inmates ONLY get novels for $10.00 per book!

Titles		*Fee*
Shyt List		$15.00
Shyt List 2		$15.00
Pitbulls In A Skirt		$15.00
Pitbulls In A Skirt 2		$15.00
Pitbulls In A Skirt 3		$15.00
Pitbulls In A Skirt 4		$15.00
Victoria's Secret		$15.00
Poison		$15.00
Poison 2		$15.00
Hell Razor Honeys		$15.00
Hell Razor Honeys 2		$15.00
A Hustler's Son 2		$15.00
Black And Ugly As Ever		$15.00
Year of The Crack Mom		$15.00
The Face That Launched a Thousand Bullets		$15.00
The Unusual Suspects		$15.00
Miss Wayne & The Queens of DC		$15.00
Year of The Crack Mom		$15.00
Paid in Blood		$15.00
Shyt List III		$15.00
Shyt List IV		$15.00
Raunchy		$15.00
Raunchy 2		$15.00
Raunchy 3		$15.00
Jealous Hearted		$15.00
Quita's Dayscare Center		$15.00
Quita's Dayscare Center 2		$15.00
Shyt List V		$15.00
Deadheads		$15.00
Pretty Kings		$15.00
Drunk & Hot Girls		$15.00
Hersband Material		$15.00
Upscale Kittens		$15.00
Wake & Bake Boys		$15.00
Young & Dumb		$15.00
Tranny 911		$15.00
First Comes Love Then Comes Murder		$15.00
Young & Dumb: Vyce's Getback		$15.00

Please add $4.00 per book for shipping and handling.
The Cartel Publications * P.O. Box 486 * Owings Mills * MD * 21117

Name: _____

Address:_____

City/Slate:_____

Contact # & Email:_____

Please allow 5-7 business days for delivery. The Cartel is not responsible for prison orders rejected.

Personal Checks Are Not Accepted.